BEGIN AGAIN

Cover Design and Interior Formatting by Nuno Moreira, NM DESIGN

ISBN Paperback: 979-8-9986769-0-1

ISBN eBook: 979-8-9986769-1-8

BEGIN AGAIN

D.F. MADDOX

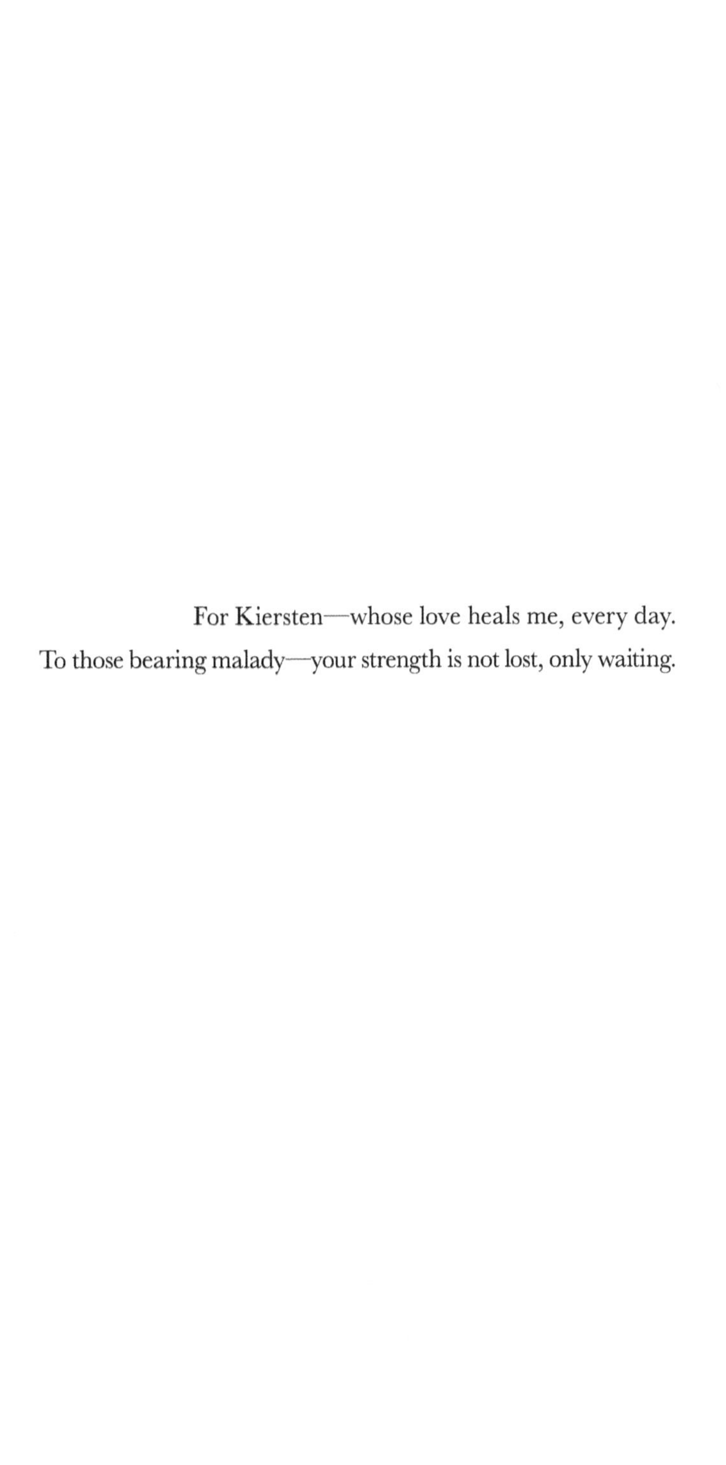

For Kiersten—whose love heals me, every day.

To those bearing malady—your strength is not lost, only waiting.

PART I

ALONE

CHAPTER 1

My Dearest Bjorn,

The morning light drapes itself across the windowpane, soft as the grey moth's wing. I watch it stretch, reaching for the corners of this room we shared for so many months. It makes me think of us, how we too stretched and reached, how we filled the sanguine spaces with the mosaic of our lives.

If you are reading this, it means I have gone ahead of you. Don't be afraid, my love. I have only stepped into the meadow beyond the one we know, where the grasses sway as if they remember our laughter, and the sky bends low to kiss the earth. I can almost hear the gentle beacon of eternity calling me home. But before I leave you entirely, there are words I must place into your hands, as carefully as I once placed them into your heart.

Do not worry if the edges of your memories blur, if names and days scatter like leaves on an autumn wind. Our love was never confined to such small boxes. It is stitched into the fabric of things—the creak of the old oak floor beneath your feet, the scent of lilacs in spring, the sound of the rain tapping softly against the roof. You carry it even now, though you may not remember the story behind each thread. But you are the lucky one; you will live on.

There are so many things I could tell you—about the

nights we stayed awake until dawn, about the dances while cooking chorizo carbonara, about the way your smile could stir the crested lark to song. But perhaps you don't need those details. Perhaps it is enough to say that this life has been sweeter because of you. And I'm sorry things fell apart. Time is bitter tea.

When you find yourself standing in the garden, as I know you will, I want you to look at the sunflowers. I planted them for you. Did you know they turn their faces to follow the sun? Just like you have always done, my love. Even when the shadows crept long across our days, you found a way to seek the brightness. You found a way to survive. Do that for me now. Be the sunflower.

And there is Tora, our loyal dog, with her golden coat and watchful eyes. She will keep you company in the sullen hours, nudging you with her nose when she senses your melancholy, lying by your feet as though she knows her purpose is to guard your heart. Let her be your companion, Bjorn. Let her remind you that even in loneliness, there is warmth to be found, a shared life to hold onto.

And if ever the fog of forgetting seems too thick, hold this letter in your hands. Let it be a compass. Let it remind you of the way we held each other, the way we laughed until tears came, the way we lived. Let it remind you that even in parting, I remain. In the dim hum of the world, in the reflections of the mountain's spine, in the space between breaths, I am there.

Do not weep for what is lost. Instead, my darling, carry me forward in your own way, in your own time. Love the days that come, the small and tender moments that still await you. You are not alone, even if the shadows of memory whisper otherwise.

I loved you then, I love you now, and I will love you in all the ways the world allows—even when the world is different than the one we knew.

Always yours,

Em

TEN YEARS AFTER "THESEUS"

The air near the river was cooler, a thin mist rising as the dawn broke open across the treetops. Bjorn crouched on the bank, the line of his fishing rod taut in his hands. Tora sat beside him, her ears pricked forward, her flaxen coat glinting faintly in the muted sunshine. The river's song was balanced and unhurried, weaving itself into the pulse of his being.

He tugged gently, the rod bending as he reeled in his catch: a small trout, glistening and vibrant, as if it carried the essence of the stream within its scales. Bjorn worked with practiced and calloused hands, a subtle precision born from years of necessity. Tora's nose twitched as she watched, her presence an anchor.

"Not bad, eh, girl?" Bjorn said, holding the trout up to the sky. Tora tilted her head, her eyes narrowing slightly as if appraising his work. "You think we should throw it back?" he asked, chuckling softly.

Tora let out a low chuff through her nose, then leaned forward to sniff the fish before retreating, her expression as dignified as only a dog's could be.

"I'll take that as a no," Bjorn murmured, a slight smile playing at his lips as he returned the fish to the basket. "You've got high standards, I see. More of a salmon girl, eh? None around here today, sorry love." Bjorn placed the day's catch on racks and hung on lines for salting and drying. He protected the fish from flies using well-worn nets.

The cabin was not far, tucked into the embrace of the forest, its walls marked by the seasons—weathered wood darkened by rain, a roof patched with care, lichen traversing the posterior wall.

Inside, the space was simple: a table worn smooth by time, a hearth that carried the mineral scent of ash and pine laced with dried brook trout, and a single shelf lined with books whose spines he often traced but seldom opened, fearing they'd evoke memories of a tortured past he could not reckon with. To him, words could be an iron maiden.

Bjorn moved through his days like this, each moment a thread in a tapestry he could not always recall. The seizures came as reveries, slipping in without warning, leaving pieces of the world scattered in their wake like black holes. Deja vu came and went like celestial bodies in the night sky. Yet Tora's watchful eyes never left him. She was there, always, as if she could sense the currents beneath his skin.

When morsels of fish were cleaned and set to cook over the fire, Bjorn stepped outside, the river still murmuring in the distance. The forest stretched endlessly before him, a cathedral of green and gold.

"What do you think, girl?" he said, glancing at Tora, who had trotted ahead to sniff a patch of ferns, then sporadically scratched her flanks with her incisors. She turned back to him, her tail wagging in sluggish, deliberate arcs, as if weighing the question.

"You like it here as much as I do, don't you?"

Tora padded closer, her nose nudging his leg. Her eyes

seemed to speak—contentment, an unspoken agreement that this place, for now, was enough. Bjorn ran a hand over her head, the motion as familiar as the great cormorant's silent vigil by the river's shore.

He inhaled deeply. Tora barked at him. But the scent of earth and moss filling his lungs lightened him, and for a fleeting moment, the fog within his mind lifted. Then he closed his eyes and let the world hold him as his knees buckled and his body vibrated like guitar strings. And Tora, ever faithful, pressed her head against his leg, grounding him once more.

*　*　*

Bjorn did not remember when the dreams began, or when they stopped being dreams at all. Some nights, they came in fragments—a flash of yellow light, the sharp crack of ice breaking underfoot, a voice calling his name, or his own eyes staring back at him. Other nights, the dreams held the weight of memory, heavy and undeniable, dragging him through moments he could no longer place.

This morning, it was the woman's voice that lingered, echoing in the serenity of the cabin. He turned the thought over like a smooth stone in his mind, but the edges refused to sharpen. Her voice was sweet like clementine sorbet and port wine, her laugh irresistible like a white sand beach after a murky winter. Tora watched him from her place by the door, her head tilted slightly, as though she too could hear the echoes.

He shook himself free of the haze and reached for his boots. There was work to be done—the kind of work that tethered him to the present, to the tangible. The axe leaned against the cabin wall, its blade dull from overuse. He picked it up, feeling the weight settle into his grip, and made his way toward the woodpile.

The rhythm of the axe splitting logs was practiced, familiar. Each swing sent a jolt through his body, a grounding force that pushed back against the fog. Tora circled nearby, her nose close to the ground, ears flicking at every flutter of the underbrush. A wiggle of her snout as the forest air gusted through the nearby field. The forest was alive with its own brilliant symphony—the chirp of the pine crickets, the distant warbling of a song thrush, the creak of branches shifting in the zephyr.

"Hear that?" Bjorn said, pausing mid-swing to look at Tora. "It's too quiet out there."

Tora froze, her body tense, her ears swiveling toward the shadows at the tree line. Her stance was cautious but unwavering, and Bjorn knew better than to ignore her instincts.

"You're not just humoring me, are you, girl?" he said, his voice low.

Tora turned her head to look at him, her amber eyes sharp and serious. She let out a soft woof, almost as if to say, "I'm not."

Bjorn nodded, gripping the axe a little tighter as he scanned the forest. Whatever was out there, he trusted her to sense it first.

* * *

Bjorn's grip on the axe remained true as his eyes scanned the shadows beneath the towering pines. Tora's tail had gone still, her focus fixed on the dark space beyond the tree line. Bjorn took a prolonged step forward, the forest's idleness now pressing in on him, murky and heavy.

"What is it, girl?" he murmured, his voice barely more than a whisper. Tora didn't move, but her ears twitched, her body coiled like a spring ready to release.

A breeze stirred the branches, bringing with it the faintest sound—a rustling that wasn't quite the wind, nor the usual scurry of a black squirrel or magpie. It was heavier, deliberate. Bjorn felt his pulse hasten as his senses sharpened, his awareness narrowing to the space ahead. The forest no longer felt like a cathedral of green but a vast, unknowable labyrinth.

"Stay close," he said, though the words felt unnecessary. Tora pressed closer to his side, her presence warm against his leg. Bjorn tightened his grip on the axe, the worn handle familiar in his calloused hands.

Then, just as suddenly as it had started, the sound ceased. The silence that followed was sharper than any noise, a void that seemed to pull at the edges of his thoughts. Bjorn exhaled steadily, his breath clouding in the cool air. Whatever had been there was gone—or perhaps it had only retreated deeper into the forest, watching from a distance.

"Come on," he said finally, his voice louder now as if to dispel the tension. "Let's head back before the storm rolls in." But even as he turned toward the cabin, his eyes gripped the tree line, and he couldn't shake the feeling that something—or someone—had been watching.

Back at the cabin, the fire crackled and danced in the hearth, its light pirouetted across the rough-hewn walls. Bjorn sat at the small table, his hands wrapped around a mug of pine needle tea, the warmth grounding him. Tora lay at his feet, her head resting on her paws, though her ears flicked at the slightest noise from outside.

"What do you think, girl?" Bjorn said, breaking the silence. "Could've been a deer, right? Or a fox. Nothing we haven't seen before."

Tora lifted her head slightly, her amber eyes meeting his with an expression that felt far too knowing for a dog. She huffed softly, which seemed to say, "If that's what you want to believe."

Bjorn chuckled, though the sound was hollow. "You're probably right. I should listen to you more often." He reached down to scratch behind her ears, and she leaned into his hand, her tail giving a proud wag.

The momentary levity faded as Bjorn's gaze drifted to the window. The forest beyond was a wall of black, the faint outline of trees barely visible against the night sky. He sipped his tea, the bitterness grounding him, and tried to push the unease from his mind.

But the dreams came again that night, more vivid than before. The flash of yellow light burned brighter, the crack of ice sharper, the voice calling his name more insistent. His own eyes stared back at him, pale and stygian—familiar and unfamiliar. Bjorn woke with a start, his breath coming in ragged gasps. Tora was at his side instantly, her nose nudging his arm, her low whine filled with concern.

"I'm okay," he murmured, though the words felt unconvincing even to himself. He ran a hand through his hair, damp with sweat, and leaned back against the headboard.

Tora climbed onto the bed, her presence a reassuring weight against his side.

As he stared at the ceiling, the fragments of the dream replayed in his mind, refusing to fade. The voice had been so clear, so familiar, yet he couldn't place it. And the light—there was something about it that made his chest ache with an unnamed longing.

"Tomorrow," he said softly, his voice barely audible over Tora's steady breathing. "We'll figure it out. Whatever's out there, we'll find it."

Tora shifted closer, her head resting on his chest, and the heat of her presence said, "We will."

And in the quiet of the cabin, with the forest stretching endlessly beyond, Bjorn let himself drift back into uneasy sleep.

*   *   *

Bjorn woke to the first traces of dawn creeping through the window. The morning sun, dappled and hesitant, spilled onto the wooden floor. Tora was already awake, her ears perked, her gaze fixed on the door. She let out a low, almost imperceptible grumble when Bjorn stirred. Then she nuzzled her head into his armpit, staring lovingly at him.

"You're up early, girl," Bjorn muttered, sitting up and stretching his arms. His joints popped in protest, a reminder of the years spent hauling firewood, fishing for brook trout, and carving out a life in this untamed expanse.

"Something on your mind?"

Tora didn't answer, of course, but her tail wagged once,

leisurely and deliberate. It was a well-worn script, and Bjorn knew his lines—she was anxious but patient, her way of saying there was nothing to fear yet, only something to note. He rubbed the sleep from his eyes and swung his legs over the edge of the bed, his bare feet finding the rutty floorboards.

Breakfast was simple: a piece of yesterday's fish, warmed over the embers in the hearth, and a hunk of bread that had grown dense and chewy with age. Bjorn ate without much mind for savoring his meal, Tora at his side, her eyes sharp and attentive.

"Hunting today," he said aloud, breaking the silence. "We'll see if we can track that buck I spotted near the creek last week." Tora's tail thumped against the floor in approval.

The forest was alive with its own heartbeat, the wind purring through the pines, the distant chatter of birds breaking the stillness. Bjorn moved with care, his steps measured, his eyes scanning the ground for any sign of tracks. The bow slung over his shoulder felt heavy but reassuring, its seedy wood a companion in these solitary ventures.

Tora ranged ahead, her nose close to the ground, sniffing out the trail. She moved with purpose, her aureate back blending into the columns of sunshine filtering through the trees. Every so often, she would pause, her ears swiveling toward some unseen sound, before continuing forward.

Bjorn knelt by a patch of soft earth, his fingers tracing the faint outline of a hoofprint. "Looks fresh," he murmured, glancing up at Tora. She was already watching him, her burnished eyes gleaming with understanding. "This way, then."

They followed the trail deeper into the forest, the canopy

above growing denser, harder to traverse, difficult to see. The air here was cooler, tinged with the earthy scent of liverwort and damp leaves. Bjorn's breath puffed in tiny clouds as he moved, his senses attuned to every snap of a twig, every rustle of leaves.

The trail led them to a small clearing, the grass flattened where the deer had bedded down. Bjorn crouched low, his eyes narrowing as he scanned the area. The tracks were clear, leading toward a cluster of birches on the far side of the clearing. He motioned for Tora to stay close, his movements measured and vigilant.

They pressed on, the forest growing subdued with each step. The silence was unnerving, heavy with the weight of expectation. Bjorn's grip on the bow tightened as he ducked under a low-hanging branch, his eyes fixed on the trail ahead.

Then, a sound—a sharp crack, like a branch snapping underfoot. Bjorn froze, his heart pounding in his chest. Tora's body stiffened beside him, her ears pinned back, her gaze fixed on the dense underbrush ahead.

Bjorn raised a hand, signaling for Tora to stay put. He nocked an arrow, the string drawing tense as he aimed toward the sound. He held his breath, and narrowed his focus. The forest seemed to follow his lead, the seconds stretching into eternity.

A shadow moved, low and swift, barely visible through the underbrush. Bjorn's grip faltered for a moment, his mind racing. Too small for the buck. Too fast for a fox. His pulse quickened as he adjusted his aim, his muscles tense.

Before he could release the arrow, the shadow vanished, melting into the forest as if it had never been there. Bjorn held his stance for a moment longer, his eyes scanning the trees, his ears straining for any sound.

"Nothing," he muttered, lowering the bow. His voice sounded hollow in the stillness. Tora let out a low growl, her body still tense, her gaze fixed on the spot where the shadow had disappeared.

"Come on," Bjorn said, his voice low. "Let's keep moving."
Then.
Suddenly.

As they entered a clearing—a whirring, zipping, droning noise crescendoed. A massive emperor dragonfly appeared, like nothing Bjorn had ever seen—perhaps, his mind deceived him? *Almost thirty centimeters long,* Bjorn thought.

Bjorn nocked an arrow, and Tora barked.

The dragonfly landed on a boulder in the clearing and its wings paused their flutter. Staring at Bjorn with crystalline eyes, it seemed to deliver an omen. A warning. Nature shifted, mutated, evolved in mysterious ways—ways beyond Bjorn, beyond what the human mind could understand.

"How peculiar, magnificent even, I suppose… huh Tora?" Tora leaned in closer by his side, and bared her teeth.

"It's beautiful." The sun glinted on its cerulean alien thorax.

Then, its wings beat and thrummed like war drums. Bjorn caught a metallic scent, a rotten sweetness.

"Ugh, what is that?" he asked aloud, Tora's nose already in the air, shifting like mad trying to find the source.

The dragonfly ascended and disappeared as it climbed into the sky.

"Careful now, Tora. The woods aren't finished with us

yet. That felt wrong."

They trekked onward, deeper. As they passed columns of fat spruce, Bjorn couldn't shake the feeling that they were not alone. The trail grew fainter, the tracks harder to follow, as if the deer they tracked had vanished into thin air. The forest seemed to close in around them, the shadows deepening, the day fading to evening.

Bjorn's breath came quicker now, his senses on edge. The wilderness had always been unpredictable, but today it felt different—charged with a certain intensity, as if the forest itself was watching.

Then. Suddenly.

They heard it.

Somewhere in the distance.

Just out of sight.

The sound of crackling leaves broke the forest stillness like a terror in the night.

*　*　*

Bjorn stepped back, head on a swivel. His boots crunched softly on a bed of dry needles.

A small, trembling form emerged from behind a cluster of ferns. There, nestled in a sun-dappled clearing, was a bear cub—its russet fur moistened from the underbrush, and its wide, uncertain eyes reflecting both wonder and a solemn plea for unbridled conservatorship.

The forest, ever the silent sentinel, seemed to lean in closer to witness this, a creature with the propensity for ungodly might dazzling Bjorn and Tora with a tenuous moment of vulnerability.

Tora leapt forward, yelping like an alarm system imbibing on its intruder, until finding her grounding in some folk empathy binding her to a fellow beast. In a gentle act of unspoken communion, Tora approached the cub with the delicate insistence of a summer rain. Then she licked at the creature's peart ear. The cub's response was immediate and unreserved—a playful roll onto its back, exposing a tender trust that warmed the chill of Bjorn's cautious heart.

The precious interlude between bear and dog passed, untimely and soon forgotten. Bjorn's pulse quickened as he weighed the fragile peace before him. The forest, in its eternal cadence of life and survival, soughed with caution. He knew too well the fierce protective instincts that ruled these wild domains—a mother bear's fury strikes with the sudden force of a breaking thunderhead. Yet the cub's unassuming persistence, its small paws padding after them with an almost hymn-like devotion, stirred in him a reluctant compassion.

Each step back toward the cabin was measured and laden with uncertainty. The cub trotted beside them, its presence a gentle disruption to the familiar rhythm of their solitary life. The choir of bear, dog, and man, gliding over root, branch, and loam, sang from the canopy to the gilded hillside. Earthworm and mycelium alike sensed the fated trio shake mother nature's hand; in all its unpredictable splendor, she sometimes extended kindness even to the most unexpected wanderers.

The three arrived at the cabin as thirsty as a thicket of desert willows. Tora rushed for the river and slurped up a pint. The bear cub clumsily approached the river, its rear foot catching the bulge of a spruce root. He let out a meager cry and Bjorn rushed to his attendance.

"You stub your toe, little guy?" Bjorn tentatively rested a hand on his pristine head. "It happens to the best of us."

The bear cub sat up and rushed to Tora's side for a drink. The two lapped up the cool water, their reflections rippling in the current. Tora splashed at the surface with a playful paw, sending shimmering droplets toward the cub. The little bear flinched, then snorted in delight. It swatted at the river, its wide paws making a larger splash.

Bjorn chuckled, stepping onto the rocky shore. "You two are gonna make a mess of yourselves," he warned, but there was no real scolding in his voice—just amusement.

Undeterred, Tora lowered herself into the shallows, letting the water swirl around her legs. She'd never minded getting wet, and the summer heat made the river feel more inviting than ever. The bear cub watched, hesitant, then dipped a paw in. The cool sensation made him pause. His ears perked up, and then, in a burst of enthusiasm, he stomped both paws into the water, sending a spray of droplets into the air.

Tora yipped and jumped back, but then, eyes glinting with mischief, she whirled and sent a wave right back at him. The cub let out a surprised grunt before retaliating with a full-bodied splash.

Bjorn shielded his face as water sprayed up toward him. "Hey! Some of us are trying to stay dry!" He stepped back, but there was no stopping them now.

"I hate to ruin your fun, but I can't shake this feeling we're being watched." Bjorn's neck tensed.

With a loud plop, the cub landed belly-first into the river. A moment of stillness hung in the air, then—grumble. A snort. And then a delighted chuff.

The bear cub was laughing. Or at least, something close to it.

Tora tilted her head before bounding over and splashing alongside him. Bjorn watched from the shore, arms crossed, a lopsided grin on his face.

"Well," he mused, "so much for just getting a drink."

Bjorn sighed, running a hand through his damp hair. "You two are gonna be a real handful, aren't you?"

But as he watched them—Tora flopping onto her side in the sun, the cub rolling onto its back with a happy grunt—he knew their new friend couldn't stay. For his cabin was no place for a bear. Even if his mother didn't come looking, the beast would outgrow their humble abode by next winter.

While weighing his options, he opened the letter.

It had been there for as long as he could remember—or, rather, for as long as his memory began. Tucked in the back of the dresser, beneath a woolen scarf he'd never worn, inside a drawer that stuck when the air was damp. The paper was soft with age, the fold lines brittle. His name was written on the outside in a looping script, familiar and foreign all at once.

"Bjorn."

He read it aloud, just to hear it. Just to feel it in his mouth. The sound settled strangely in his chest.

He eased onto the edge of his bed, the wood creaking beneath his weight. Outside, the river droned, the wind shifted through the spruce, and the bear cub snuffled in its sleep. Tora stirred but did not awaken.

His fingers worked the fold apart, careful, though he didn't know why. The ink was slightly smudged in places.

The last words were damp from his tears that fell after each time he read the letter:

...I loved you then, I love you now, and I will love you in all the ways the world allows—even when the world is different than the one we knew.

Always yours,

Em

Bjorn let the letter rest in his lap, his hands gripping the edges as though it might vanish if he let go. He stared at the words, waiting for recognition to strike, for warmth to bloom in his chest, for the shape of a life—his life—to fill the hollow spaces in his mind.

But nothing came.

Tora shifted, lifting her head, sensing something in the silence. The bear cub let out another soft huff in its sleep. The river moved on, unconcerned.

Bjorn folded the letter carefully, smoothing the creases before tucking it back into the drawer.

He did not remember her. But once—once—he must have.

CHAPTER 2

The lion is King
The tiger is Tsar
The jaguar is Tlatoan
The leopard is Mwami
The shark is Basileus
The dragon is Huángdì
But the bear,
The bear is the
Mother of them all.

A few days prior, the morning sun, pale as a pearl, rose slothfully over the rolling hills, gilding the ancient pines and great boulders with a warm glow. The forest stirred, shaking off the mantle of night with the rustle of wind through trembling leaves. Beneath the towering firs, where the scent of damp earth and pine resin wove densely through the cool air, a bear and her cub awoke.

The mother bear, broad and golden-brown, lifted her heavy head and exhaled in the crisp air, searching for the scent of movement. Her eyes, dark pools of wisdom, turned to the small, round creature still curled at her side.

The cub, soft-furred and clumsy, yawned widely, revealing tiny teeth, and stretched his limbs with the slow, sprawling ease of one who has never known fear. Then the mother stretched her body long, as if to say, "Awaken my child, for the earth breathes anew."

"Mam, fair dawn to you."

"The fairest, mmmm, the day's first breath. My belly roars for river's scale-bearers," she replied with a nuzzle of her snout against his. "Does your belly yearn, cub? The river's silver awaits the mouths of the young." She licked his ears and head, grooming him for the day.

They set forth through the undergrowth, her massive paws pressing into the damp loam, leaving prints deep and true. The cub bounded ahead, snuffling at ferns and snapping playfully at a drifting brush-footed butterfly, his small form a lively contrast to his mother's steady gait. The river called to them—a distant murmur that rose to a rushing song as they approached. The water, clear as polished quartz, tumbled over basalt and umbre stones, whispering its eternal story to the trees that leaned close to listen.

"Do you hear, little one?" She perked her head up, to force his attention. "What moves there, in the hush?" He looked at her. "The swift-finned folk come thick and fast! Steel your hunger, little one." She smiled.

At the river's edge, the mother bear took her place, standing still as stone, the power in her limbs held in perfect stillness. Her dark eyes scanned the silver dance of fish below, the salmon moving like flickering torches beneath the current. Then, with a suddenness that defied her immense form, she struck—a flash of golden fur, a spray of water. When she lifted her head again, the fish, sleek and glistening, struggled in her grasp.

The cub watched with wide, curious eyes. He waded in after her, his tiny paws slipping on the wet stones, his belly brushing against the shallows. He lunged clumsily at the darting fish, but his attempts yielded nothing but laughter—like chuffs from his mother.

She nudged him with her great nose, and he squeaked, indignant but undeterred.

"Steady, young hunter. Wait for their dance with the current. When they breach the water's skin, open wide and seize your gift." She clenched her jaw with mighty force as a salmon leapt from the river.

Again and again, he tried, until at last, by luck or instinct, his small mouth struck true. He lifted his first catch, triumphant, and paraded it proudly before his mother, who rumbled with amusement.

As the sun climbed high, they moved to a meadow where the scent of summer flowers punched heady, and the ground was soft with moss. The mother stretched, rolling onto her back, and with a great sigh, settled into the warmth. The cub took this as an invitation, pouncing upon her massive belly, his tiny claws digging playfully into her woolly fur. She swatted at him with careful tenderness, rolling him over, nudging him with a great paw. He tumbled, laughing in the way only cubs can, and for a time, they played, a world of their own beneath the vast blue sky.

Then the world changed.

A sound—low, guttural, unnatural—rolled through the trees. The mother bear froze, every muscle locked, her ears pricked. The cub, oblivious, continued gnawing at her paw until she let out a deep, warning growl. Instinct stirred in him then, a primal knowledge as old as the earth itself. He stilled, his small body pressing close to hers.

The wind shifted, carrying a scent that did not belong—a scent sharp with hunger, with something beyond the ordinary threats of the forest. From the specters between the trees, eyes glowed—yellow and patient, calculating. A wolf pack? No, something more. Something unseen but felt, as if the night itself had crept too close before the sun had set.

"To my shadow, cub! Waste no breath." She roared. The mother launched onto her hind legs, her full height a mountain of golden fur and power. Her cub, Sild, retreated, cowering.

Her roar split the silence, reverberating through the valley like rolling thunder. Whatever lurked in the shadows hesitated. The cub slunk behind his mother, pressing into the warmth of her fur. And then—just as swiftly as it had come— the presence withdrew, fading into the undergrowth as though it had never been there at all.

The mother bear rumbled low, a reassurance, and nosed at her cub until he stirred again. The moment passed, but the air carried its ghost.

That night, beneath the great cloak of darkness, the cub slept beside his mother once more. The stars wheeled overhead, silent and watching, and the wind wove its hushed lullaby through the branches. The cub drifted into sleep, safe beneath his mother's steady breath.

But when he woke, the world was different.

The space beside him was empty.

The ground was cold where his mother had lain. The

wind had shifted, and with it, the scent of her was fading. The trees stood tall and indifferent, the river murmured on, oblivious. The cub lifted his small head, his dark eyes searching, his breath hitching.

A soundless void pressed against him, redolent with the absence of what should have been there. He whimpered, a small and lonely sound swallowed by the vastness of the forest. He stood on trembling legs, turned in circles, sniffed at the air. There was no blood, no sign of struggle—only emptiness.

The night had taken her.

The cub sat back on his haunches, staring into the trees, waiting. The stars gleamed cold and distant. The wind whispered endless secrets.

And the forest, ancient and knowing, watched in silence. Well, only until Bjorn arrived.

CHAPTER 3

My dog's face
As she slumbers
Makes me think
A god could exist

Not because of
providence
Or shema yisrael
Or moksha

Because when she calls
I am prone, scratching her belly
When she coos, I kiss her ear
And sometimes she places a paw
On my hand
As if to say
You are forgiven
For all that
You carry within
Your neck and shoulders

She will never tire
Of the songs I compose
In her honor
Like one almighty

Spirit is not something
Carrying you into the next plane
Spirit is something
Clinging you to this one

Bjorn was chopping wood near the cabin when the sound of the wind shifted, accompanied by a visceral clenching in his gut. He stilled, axe hovering mid-air. The rustling wasn't random—it was rhythmic. A pattern. Words. He shook his head, dismissing it. But later that night, as he lay awake in bed, he swore he heard his name carried through the trees.

In his deep slumber, Bjorn dreamt of a house he did not remember but somehow belonged to him. The doors stood open, wind slipped through, the scent of rain on stone, of something floral but ashen. The floorboards bent under his step as if expecting his return. His fingers traced the frame of a doorway, and the wood was warm, as though someone else had just passed through.

A woman's voice drifted from the far end of the hall—not calling, not pleading, just existing, like a thread woven through the air. He did not move toward it, nor away. He only stood there, feeling the house settle around him, the walls holding a history his mind refused to give back. He woke, and his hands were empty, but the scent remained.

He shook off the dream. Tora licked his face. He scratched her behind the ear. The bear cub already woken, rummaged through the scant pantry, and snacked on the dried herring Bjorn saved from a prior trek to the coast.

*   *   *

The river was different today. Bjorn felt it before he saw it, the way the air thickened near the banks, the way the current chorused rather than mumbled its musings. The mist clung low to the surface, threading through the reeds like something half-alive, stirring at the edges of his perception.

He knelt at the river's edge, hands clasping the damp stones, then dipped his hands into the water. He expected the usual bite of cold, it was a glacial tributary, so an icy shock should have numbed his skin, even in summer. But it didn't come.

The water was warm.

His breath hitched. He pulled his hands back, shaking off the droplets, rubbing his palms together as if the friction might make sense of what he had felt. He flexed the muscles in his hands. His skin was dry almost instantly, as if the water had never truly touched him.

Bjorn hesitated, then leaned forward again, dipping his hands deeper. The warmth pulsed this time, gentle but undeniable. It wasn't the false heat of his own body adjusting to the cold—it was external, radiating, aware.

The river recognized him.

The thought came unbidden, sending a ripple of unease down his spine. The current shifted as he exhaled, a slow, deliberate movement that did not match the wind or the flow of the stream further upstream. It spun around his wrists, pressing, holding.

Testing.

Bjorn yanked his hands back, his breath ragged. He rocked onto his heels, scanning the treeline, searching for some explanation. The world remained as it had always been—silent, indifferent. But the river had changed. Or maybe, it had always been like this, and he was only just now able to perceive it.

His reflection shimmered in the water, its edges blurring, distorting. For a moment, he swore his eyes looked different. Darker. Deeper. As though the water was seeing something beyond his flesh, beneath his skin.

A sharp bark cut through the stillness.

Bjorn jerked upright, turning toward the cabin. Tora stood at the treeline, her body tense, ears pinned back. She had been watching him.

He wiped his hands on his coat, ignoring the way they no longer felt wet. Ignoring the way the river still pulsed behind him, waiting. He did not return to it, even though the river called to him. And worse, he wasn't sure if he wanted to resist.

Shaking off the moment—Bjorn released a deep sigh. "I guess we must find an elk today, huh? The little guy loves herring," Bjorn said, referring to the bear cub. "Should we call him Sild, huh Tora?" Tora woofed in response, she agreed.

The morning air was pungent with pine and damp earth as Bjorn waded past through larch and fir tree, his breath controlled, his muscles loose. Tora padded close, her tail low, ears flicking to the soft cacophony of unseen things beyond the trees. Sild lumbered beside them, his stout legs clumsy but determined, his nose sniffing at every new scent, his small black eyes round with curiosity.

Bjorn had been tracking the elk for a week now, to no avail, reading the signs in the earth, the way broken twigs and torn moss muttered their direction. It had passed through the glade near the river, its hooves pressing deep into the soft mud. The trail was fresh.

He knelt, fingers brushing over the impressions. "Big one," he murmured, mostly to himself.

Tora sniffed the ground, then looked up at him, her amber eyes sharp.

Bjorn nodded. "You think it's alone?"

She gave a short, deliberate puff—maybe, maybe not.

Sild watched them, then shoved his wet nose into the print, snorting at the smell before looking back at Bjorn expectantly.

Bjorn chuckled, ruffling the dense fur behind the cub's ears. "Yeah, yeah. I know. You're hungry."

Sild let out a soft huff, settling back on his haunches. His belly was round, filled with this morning's stolen herring, but already, the cub wanted more.

They pressed forward, the rhythm of their movements blending into the forest's pulse. The towering pines leaned close, intonating in a language older than humankind, older than names. The earth was dark, rich, giving. Each step felt as though they were walking within something alive— breathing, watching, waiting.

The elk's trail wove deeper into the forest, crossing between boulders draped in velvet moss. The air shifted, the scent changing. Tora halted first, her body stiff. Sild nearly stumbled into her. Bjorn caught himself against a tree, scanning the ground.

Not the elk.

Something else.

Bear scat.

Fresh.

His jaw tensed. He crouched, examining the dark pile. The steam still rose from it, floating into the cool air. If female, perhaps Sild's mother, or a new guardian for his adoption. If male, they'd all be lunchmeat.

Bjorn exhaled methodically, his fingers brushing against his belt where his bowie knife sat snug. He had lived in these woods long enough to know the rules—give the big ones their space, move carefully, do not tempt fate.

Tora let out a low growl, her tail rigid.

Bjorn placed a hand on her head. "Easy, girl. We don't know where he is yet."

Sild, oblivious to caution, sniffed at the scat, then sneezed violently. He reeled back, shaking his snout in absolute disgust.

Bjorn smothered a laugh. "Yeah, welcome to the wild, little guy."

But something in the air was wrong. The forest had gone still. The wind had hushed. Even the birds, ever insistent in their morning gossip, had silenced their chatter.

Bjorn felt it in his bones first—a shifting, an awareness.

And then he saw it.

The alpha male bear emerged from the trees like a moving shadow, its mass larger than any creature had a right to be.

Muscles rippled beneath its muggy fur, dark as storm clouds. Its breath billowed in the cool air, deep and measured, its black eyes locking onto Bjorn's with the weight of something ancient.

Tora barked once, sharp and urgent. Sild whined, his small body pressing into Bjorn's leg.

Bjorn did not move.

The bear studied them, nostrils flaring. Its head was high, its stance deliberate. A test. It wanted to see if he would yield, if he would flee.

But then something else came.

A sharp, burning light inside Bjorn's skull.

The world tilted.

His mind lost and body convulsed like shifting tectonic plates.

The pain came in waves—his muscles clenched, his breath stopped, and then the earth fell away.

He was floating.

A bright light, a yellow warmth. A voice he should know but couldn't place. Lips he kissed before. Skin that smelled like an evening of bergamot, clementine sorbet, and port wine.

Then—

The world slammed back into focus.

The ground was beneath him again, his body still trembling from the aftershock of the seizure. His hands dug into the dirt, nails packed with soil. His breath was ragged.

Tora whined, nudging his face frantically. Sild let out distressed grunts, pacing around him, his small paws shuffling in the loam.

Bjorn blinked, his vision struggling to right itself.

Then—

His chest clenched. He knew something was behind him. The forest spoke to him in seductive and terrifying ways. It purred and bleated in the cold darkness. Something grotesque, something sinister lurked between the pillars of wych elm.

It spoke his name on the wind. *Bjorn*. He turned.

A sound.

A high-pitched, unnatural frequency.

The alpha bear roared.

Bjorn's stomach clenched as he looked up. The massive bear had reared onto its hind legs, its maw wide, agape, saliva dripping—a soundless snarl. But it wasn't looking at Bjorn anymore.

It was looking behind him.

The orb hovered there, sleek and metallic, no larger than a man's fist. It pulsed with a strange energy, undulating like a pebble in the river, then spinning in measured, mechanical, revolutions. Upon closer inspection, Bjorn saw the surface was made of a strange living metal, pulsing with sickly blue light like a haunted fungus gnat larvae—orfelia fultoni.

Bjorn vomited. He could barely stand. Shaking.

And then, a sound.

A noise that did not belong to the earth, nor the trees, nor the sky.

A noise that tightened the bones and pressed against the lungs—a frequency sharp, invasive, otherworldly.

Bjorn winced, clamping his hands over his ears. Tora let out a yelp, flattening herself to the ground. Sild collapsed onto his belly, his small body trembling.

The bear let out a guttural roar, stepping back, its massive claws raking against the earth. It rampaged toward the orb—breaking through a thicket of mountain ash.

The orb released a noxious gas. It smelled like butyric acid, ammonia, and rot.

Bjorn gagged—holding down the boiled brook trout in his stomach.

The bear stumbled over its own feet, its powerful snout intoxicated by the gas. It struggled to regain its footing as it took a heaving swing at the orb—but it missed.

The orb fired a synthetic staple that clamped into the bear's hide. The noise from an electric pulse intensified, then the staple shocked the bear. In fear and torture, it broke through a nearby thicket.

Bjorn had never seen something so large move so fast. The beast tore through the underbrush, sending trees shaking in its wake, its growls fading into the distance.

The orb hovered for a second, humming, as if considering Bjorn, waiting, evaluating him.

Then it zipped after the bear, vanishing between the trees.

And then—

Silence.

Bjorn's pulse thundered in his ears. His breath came in uneven bursts. Tora pressed against his side, her body rigid with tension. Sild clambered onto his lap, his small frame shaking violently.

Bjorn swallowed hard.

The forest exhaled.

The wind returned, jarring the leaves. The magpies and

jackdaws hesitated, then resumed their volant chatter. The world, after its moment of pause, seemed to move again.

But Bjorn knew better.

Something had changed.

Something had arrived. Though he did not know what.

* * *

The world was still trembling when Bjorn pushed himself upright, the taste of iron lingered on his tongue. His breath came shallow and unsteady. Tora nudged at his ribs, her whines insistent, her seething eyes wide with concern. Sild huddled between his legs, his small body pressed tight against Bjorn's, his fur damp from the loamy earth.

The orb was gone. The apex bear, gone. The forest had gambled with their fate, but questioning its motivation still gathered in the back of Bjorn's throat, something unspoken pressing against the edges of his gut.

He flexed his leg muscles, testing their steadiness. "We need to move," he muttered, though neither animal needed convincing.

The elk trail was lost in the chaos, but another sign revealed itself—a scattering of stripped twigs, gnawed down to the marrow of their fibers. Bjorn recognized it immediately.

Porcupine.

Luck, it seemed, still hummed beneath his skin, though he did not know for how long.

Tora caught the scent first, her ears twitching, her nose to the damp air. Bjorn moved carefully, his steps measured against the hush of the trees. Even the wind had stilled, as if watching. The porcupine was close.

Then, there—perched low in the crook of a tree, its bristled quills rising in warning, its small beady eyes glinting with animal wariness. Bjorn didn't hesitate. He raised his bow, took a steady breath, and loosed the arrow.

A quick kill. The forest offered no time for waste.

Bjorn approached the fallen creature, his blade quick and practiced, separating what was useful from what must return to the earth. He mounted the porcupine on a sturdy branch, hoisting it like a spear over his shoulder.

A low growl of thunder rolled in the distance. Tora stiffened.

Bjorn glanced up. The sky, veiled with gathering clouds, had turned the color of old bruises. The scent of rain gnawed at his senses. The storm was coming fast.

Sild let out an uneasy snort, shuffling closer to Tora.

"Come on," Bjorn said, already stepping forward. "We need to—"

The first crack of lightning shattered the sky.

It split the heavens in a jagged, merciless streak, white and violent. Thunder followed, a deep, guttural roar that shook the gut and bones of the earth.

Sild cried out, his small body twisting in sudden panic. Before Bjorn could grab him, the cub bolted.

"No—Sild!"

The bear cub tore through the underbrush, his terror outweighing any instinct for direction.

Tora barked, loud and sharp, her body already springing into motion.

Bjorn reached out. "Tora, no—"

But she was gone.

She ran after him, disappearing into the tangled arms of the forest, swallowed whole by the wild.

Bjorn swore, adjusting his grip on the porcupine. He couldn't run—not fast enough, not through the grit of the storm, not without losing what they needed to eat.

Another crack of lightning. The wind whipped through the trees, tearing leaves from their branches, sending the world into a furious dance of movement and sound.

Bjorn clenched his teeth. Tora knew the way home. If she could not find Sild, she would return to the cabin. She had better instincts than he did.

Still, the thought of them alone in this storm made his muscles tighten.

The rain came fast. It struck him in sheets, cold and relentless, soaking through his clothes, running in rivulets down his skin. He pulled his furs tighter, bracing against the downpour, and turned toward home.

The storm did not last long, but its presence was unforgiving. By the time it began to wane, Bjorn was chilled to the bone, his fingers stiff around the wooden shaft of his makeshift spear. The trees dripped in a taunting symphony, the last remnants of rain trickling from branch to branch.

Then, the scent.

Smoke.

His pulse stilled.

No.

Not here. Not this deep in the forest. Not this close to home.

Bjorn quickened his pace, his legs heavy with exhaustion,

his breath coming in sharp bursts. He crested the final rise and stopped.

A profane echo of one's own private damnation—the cabin was aflame.

The fire roared against the night, licking at the beams, the wooden walls, the roof he had patched with his own hands. It twisted and writhed, consuming everything in its path.

Lightning must have found it. The storm, quick and brutal, had left its mark.

Bjorn's legs broke beneath him. He dropped to his knees in the wet earth, the porcupine falling from his grasp.

His home.

Everything.

Gone.

The firelight flickered against his damp skin, its warmth a cruel thing against the cold he carried inside.

The forest watched, silent once more.

He was alone, truly alone.

CHAPTER 4

Dream-keeper
Don't judge me
My ship wrecked
On your shores

In the darkness
Before the dawn
The wind was a serpent
And I could not hold on

I awoke
Spewing water
like a whale

On your beach
I crawled in the sand
Choking on kelp
Like a timid fish

Until I reached
your altar

I knew not of dreams
Only passing illusions
In an ephemeral tapestry

But I'm just looking
For somewhere to
Rest my head

If you won't
grant me this
Then I'll wander
to my past
To find you
languid like a worm
And break you

You won't see me
Holding you in my arms
Dream-keeper
I give you this one chance

The fire snapped and howled, devouring the cabin in its merciless embrace. Bjorn knelt in the damp earth, his breath shallow, the heat licking against his face even from a distance. His body had weathered storms, hunger, and time itself, but this—this hollowing loss—left him unmoored.

The cabin had been more than wood and stone. It had been a sanctuary, a refuge carved from the wilderness, a tether to whatever life he had before the forgetting. Now, it was a funeral pyre, carrying memories he could not hold onto into the blackened sky.

The storm had passed, leaving only the ruin of its passing. The trees stood tall and still, their boughs dripping with the last remnants of rain. The earth smelled of wet moss and charred timber.

Then—

A bark.

Sharp. Urgent.

Bjorn lifted his head.

Tora emerged from the trees, her Olympic gait moving her at an epic pace over branch and stone, her ribs heaving from the effort of the run. Behind her, stumbling through the shrubs, was Sild. His small, round body quivered, his fur darkened with mud, his frightened whimpers barely audible over the crackling flames.

Bjorn exhaled something like a prayer.

Tora reached him first, pressing her body into his side, whining low in her throat as if to say, "I came back. I found him."

Bjorn buried his hands in the damp fur at her neck, gripping her as if she were the only solid thing left in the world. "Good girl," he whispered, his voice raw. "Good girl, Tora."

Sild hesitated at the edge of the clearing, his small black eyes darting between Bjorn and the flames. His ears twitched at every pop and hiss from the burning wreckage.

Bjorn forced himself to his feet, his body aching, his clothes heavy with rain. He approached the cub slowly, kneeling to his level.

"Come here, little one," he murmured.

Sild hesitated only a moment before stumbling forward. Bjorn gathered the cub into his arms, his warmth a balm against the chill in Bjorn's bones. Sild let out a small, relieved grunt, pressing his wet nose into Bjorn's chest.

Bjorn closed his eyes.

They were alive. That was enough.

For now.

The fire would burn through the night, swallowing every trace of the life he had built. The forest bore witness, its great limbs stretching overhead, sheltering them even as it had failed to protect the cabin.

Bjorn turned his gaze to the treetops. The wilderness had always been unpredictable, but something had changed. The orb. The bear. The storm. It was no accident.

The forest had sent him a warning.

And he had not understood it in time.

Tora sat beside him, her body warm against his leg, her eyes reflecting the firelight with certainty. Sild nuzzled closer, his small frame still trembling.

Bjorn tightened his arms around the cub and exhaled gradually. The forest hath taken. But in its bartering, it hath given.

Tomorrow, they would begin again.

For now, they watched as the past turned to ash.

* * *

That night, they slept under the stars. Once the exhaustion had settled too deeply into his bones to be fought, the dreams found him again.

The house stood as it always did—tall and weathered, its wooden bones creaking with an ache he could not hear but could feel. The paint had been the color of cream once, but time had faded it to something between ivory and dust. The windows were dark, the door slightly ajar, as if waiting.

He knew this place. And yet, he did not.

The hillside stretched beyond the house, rolling into the distance, endless and golden, swaying with tall grasses that waltzed in the wind. Wildflowers dotted the expanse—pale blue sun-kissed fiber, the deep violet of lupines, the soft white clusters of yarrow. The scent of them drifted toward him, mingling with the crisp, sun-warmed air.

Bjorn stood at the edge of the hill, bare feet sinking into the soft, damp soil. The house behind him felt heavy, like a presence, a thing that breathed and watched. The land before him felt endless, untamed, a freedom he could almost reach.

The wind rose, lifting his hair, carrying the scent of rain—though the sky was impossibly blue, unmarred by even a wisp of cloud.

He turned toward the house, his fingers twitching at his sides. The wood grain of the door was familiar, as if his hands had traced it a thousand times before. A warmth tugged at his chest, something like longing, something like fear.

A voice—soft, warm, the phantom of laughter—carried on the breeze. It tickled his ears like a half-remembered melody, but the words were lost before he could catch them.

His feet moved of their own accord, taking him up the steps, across the threshold. The scent of lilacs and old books drifted from within.

Then—

The world tilted.

The light twisted, bleeding into something golden, something burning.

The sky darkened.

The house flickered, like a flame before the wick died.

Bjorn gasped awake.

The scent of smoke still clung to him.

He could not explain it, but the forest left him this message. He needed to find the house in his dreams. It existed, somewhere. It was his home once, he knew it. They must leave this place. Danger pulsed in the air, though he couldn't name its shape. It was just a feeling—deep, unshakable. And he had learned long ago to heed the words of the wild.

* * *

The embers of the fire still smoldered behind them, popping and crackling into the cold morning air, the last remnants of a home turned to ruin. Bjorn did not look back. He pulled his furs tighter around his shoulders, adjusted the strap of his pack, and stepped forward into the waiting forest. Tora padded beside him, silent and watchful, her ears flicking at every sound. Sild followed close, his small paws clumsy over roots and rock, but his instincts guiding him where his strength could not.

Bjorn did not know where he was going. Only that he had to go.

The house was out there, waiting for him, calling to him in

ways beyond sound. The forest knew the path before he did. It always had. He only needed to listen.

The trees spoke their warnings in the way their branches leaned, in the hush of the wind buzzing through their needles. Some paths felt wrong, the air too idle, the silence too intoxicating. Bjorn trusted the weight in his chest when it told him to turn, to climb instead of descend, to press forward when his body begged him to stop.

The land did not make this journey easy.

The first trial was the river, swollen from the storm, its waters black and fast. The bridge—little more than a fallen log—was slick with moss, half-rotted, and treacherous. Bjorn tested it with his foot, feeling the slight give beneath his weight. He exhaled sharply.

"Tora, go," he said, stepping back.

The dog hesitated for only a second before leaping onto the log, her paws light, her movements steady. She reached the far side and turned, ears pricked, waiting.

Bjorn scooped Sild into his arms, the cub letting out a surprised grunt. "Hold on, little one."

The log shifted under his step, the current below snarling at his ankles. Every step sent a shudder through the wood, but he did not stop. He would not stop.

Midway across, the log creaked—a long, sickly sound of something deciding it could no longer bear the weight.

Bjorn moved faster.

The log groaned, the sound splitting through the hush of the forest, and then—

CRACK.

The wood splintered. Bjorn lunged, throwing himself forward just as the log gave way beneath him. He clawed at the muddy riverbank, his arms straining as Sild scrambled free. Tora was there in an instant, teeth gripping the sleeve of his coat, pulling, helping, until at last, he heaved himself onto solid ground.

He lay there, panting, feeling the tremor in his limbs.

Sild, unbothered, nosed at his beard, huffing in disapproval.

Bjorn let out a winded laugh. "Yeah, yeah. I know."

They pressed on.

The forest grew denser, the light thinner. Shadows stretched long across the path, twisting over uneven ground. Gnarled roots reached out like skeletal tendrils, and Bjorn swore the trees had begun to lean inward, as if to watch, to grin devilishly.

Then came the rocks.

The land climbed steeply into the hills, forcing them onto jagged, narrow paths. The rocks were loose, the ground uncertain beneath their feet. A single misstep could send them tumbling down into the yawning dark below.

Bjorn moved carefully, testing each foothold before shifting his weight. His breath was precise, controlled. He reached for the next ledge, gripping the cold stone—

Tora barked.

A warning.

He barely had time to register the sound before the ground gave way beneath him.

The rock crumbled. Bjorn slipped, scrambling, his heart lurching into his throat. He grasped at the cliffside, but his fingers found only air.

Then—a sudden bite at his wrist.

Tora.

Her teeth locked onto his coat, pulling with every ounce of strength in her body. Bjorn gasped, his other hand catching hold of a jutting root just as Tora's grip slipped. The world tilted beneath him, his boots scraping against the crumbling edge.

Sild let out a distressed wail, pacing along the ledge above.

Bjorn gritted his teeth, forcing his weight upward, his muscles burning. With one last pull, he hauled himself onto the path, collapsing onto his back.

Tora immediately shoved her nose into his face, whining. He laughed, exhausted. "You keep saving me, girl."

Sild, apparently dissatisfied with how long it had taken, smacked Bjorn's shoulder with a clumsy paw.

Bjorn sighed. "Fine. I'll be more careful."

They moved again, trudging now, the exhaustion creeping into Bjorn's bones. Their path went on like this for another two days. Traversing terrain that challenged their every move.

The forest was testing him.

The wind carried strange sounds through the trees—low groans, rustling that did not belong to the usual stir of leaves. The scent of moldering earth thickened. Something watched, though Bjorn could not say from where.

Then, through the thinning trees, he saw it.

Not the house.

Not yet.

But the hill.

The same rolling, golden stretch he had seen in his dreams.

The house was near.

Bjorn swallowed hard, gripping the strap of his pack. He glanced at Tora, then at Sild, who blinked back at him, expectant.

The forest had not made this journey easy.

But it had brought him here.

And for that, he trusted it.

*　*　*

The hill from his dreams stretched before him in golden waves, the tall grasses swaying as if stirred by something unseen. The sight sent a tremor through his chest. This was real. The house, he could feel its presence nearby. He knew it. The forest had not deceived him.

Then—

A sound.

Low, guttural. A groan that rumbled through the trees like thunder trapped beneath the earth.

Bjorn stiffened, his fingers instinctively reaching for the knife at his belt. Tora halted beside him, ears pinned back, teeth bared.

It was a bear.

But not a hungry one.

Not a hunting one.

A dying one.

Before Bjorn could react, Sild went berserk.

The cub let out a piercing wail—a sound Bjorn had never heard from him before, raw and frantic. Then, without hesitation, he ran.

"Sild!" Bjorn shouted, but the bear cub was already gone,

tearing through the brush with a speed and desperation that sent ice through Bjorn's veins.

Tora growled and took off after him. Bjorn cursed under his breath and followed, crashing through the shrubs, pushing aside brambles that clawed at his arms, panting ragged.

The groaning grew louder, more labored.

Then, through the tangled thicket, Bjorn saw her.

A mother bear lay sprawled in the brush, her massive body heaving, gasping for air. Her fur was matted with sweat and dirt, her ribs expanding and contracting in painful, shuddering movements. Her mouth hung slightly open, revealing glistening teeth, and her eyes—dark and wild— rolled toward them as they approached.

Sild skidded to a stop, his body trembling, his pulse sharp and fast.

Bjorn hesitated, scanning the bear for injuries, expecting deep gashes, a hunter's bullet, something to explain her agony.

But there was no wound.

No blood.

Then he saw it.

Her stomach was shifting.

A gasp stuck in Bjorn's throat. "No."

It wasn't an injury—it was labor.

A bear giving birth. Here. In the open. In summer.

Impossible.

Bears gave birth in the dead of winter, deep in secluded dens, safe beneath the weight of snow and silence. This was wrong. Unnatural.

Bjorn took a cautious step back, gripping Tora's scruff and

pulling her with him. "Stay back."

But Sild did not move.

The cub inched forward, his small body drawn toward the mother, as if by instinct.

Bjorn let him go. He was not foolish enough to interfere. This was beyond him.

The mother bear let out a deep, rattling groan, her body convulsing, her massive frame arching with pain. Then, with one final, broken gasp, she gave birth.

The newborn slid onto the earth.

It did not move.

Bjorn exhaled sharply, his chest tightening. A stillborn.

The mother lifted her head, staring at the unmoving cub. A deep, guttural sound—something primeval, something grieving—rumbled from her throat. Then she coughed violently. Blood spilled from her mouth, syrupy and dark, splattering onto the ground.

And then she roared.

It was a sound Bjorn would never forget.

A final, terrible cry of agony and loss, a sound that rattled through the very bones of the world. Then—

Silence.

The mother bear collapsed, her breath faltering, her body still like dusk.

Bjorn hesitated. His pulse pounded in his ears. He had seen death before, but not like this. This was wrong.

Warily, he approached.

And then he saw what she was.

His breath caught.

The bear was not entirely a bear.

Her underbelly was wrong—an unfamiliar material, iridescent and mesh-like, nothing like the coarse fur that covered the rest of her. It was fabricated, a strange fusion of organic and synthetic, as if something had made her rather than birthed her.

Bjorn crouched, reaching out carefully, his fingers brushing against the biofabricated surface. It was warm. Not metal. Not entirely. Something in between.

"What in the hell are you?" he murmured.

The forest uttered nothing.

Tora stood beside him, her tail low, her body tense. She sensed it too—this was something that did not belong.

Sild pressed his small head against the mother's still form, letting out a quiet, sorrowful whimper.

Bjorn swallowed hard.

The bear had not just died.

She had been designed to die.

CHAPTER 5

I want to show you
I care for you
Time will heal all ills
My love
Never in the world
Have two felt this seen
Though we are but humans
As the world becomes less so
Will the coming generations
See the Matterhorn with their eyes
Or through a lens
Will the sun feel warm
Like Fenwick in July
Or will it torch the grass
Keeping the earth brittle

The road was cracked and broken, choked with weeds and the tidal creep of moss reclaiming its place. The trees that had once lined it had grown wild, their roots breaking through pavement, their branches stretching in gnarled defiance toward the sky.

Then the houses appeared.

Not one. Not just the house from his dreams.

A neighborhood—abandoned, ruined, archaic. A relic from a human civilization.

Bjorn plodded, his breath shallow, his grip tightening on the strap of his pack. Tora walked beside him, her body low, vigilant, ears twitching with every step. Sild, shaken from his grief, trailed behind, his small eyes darting between the empty homes, his nose lifting to the wind.

Bjorn swallowed hard. "What happened here?"

The houses—some leaning, some collapsed, others standing as if waiting—stared back at him with empty windows. The doors hung from rusted hinges, shadows pooling inside their frames. It had once been a place of life. Families. Footsteps on wooden porches. The hum of a distant radio.

Now, it was a graveyard.

And yet—

There.

His house.

The one from his dreams.

Bjorn's breath caught in his throat. The exact slant of the roof. The shape of the windows. The porch steps worn with use, the door slightly ajar.

He ran.

Tora chased after him, her paws barely touching the earth. Sild let out a startled grunt and followed.

Bjorn slammed his hand against the door. It swung open with ease, as if expecting him.

The smell hit him first.

Something faint but unmistakable—like warm cedar after a storm, like dogwood blossoms in late spring.

His throat tightened.

Inside, the house was frozen in time.

The walls were familiar, but the objects scattered throughout were not. Fragments of a civilization he did not recognize. Machinery rested on tables, blinking with faint, dying lights. Small devices, matte and dusty, lay discarded among rusted tools. The food in the cabinets—if it was food—was unidentifiable, sealed in strange containers, marked with words that were almost readable but bent in a way his mind couldn't grasp.

And yet, the bones of the house—its spirit—he knew.

His fingers traced the edge of the banister. The same curve from his dreams. The creak of the wood beneath his boots, exactly where he expected it. He exhaled sharply, his chest tightening with something between fear and longing.

Em.

He could almost hear her voice.

He moved through the space, drawn by something beyond reason, beyond memory. Up the stairs, down the hall, to the room that called to him.

And then—

The scent stopped him in his tracks.

The blanket, draped over the chair by the window, was faded, the fabric softened with time. But when he lifted it, pressing it to his face, the ghost of her was still there.

The delicate warmth of her skin after a long day in the sun. The lavender oil she used sparingly, rubbing it between her palms before bed. The faintest trace of wood smoke from nights spent by the fire.

His knees nearly buckled.

For a moment, all the unease, all the unanswered questions, the weight of the ruined world outside—it all vanished.

She had been here.

Once.

Tora whined, her nose pressing against Bjorn's arm.

He exhaled shakily, swallowing the lump in his throat. "I know, girl."

Then—

A crash.

Bjorn's head snapped up.

Sild.

The cub was gone.

Bjorn turned, rushing down the stairs two at a time. "Sild?" His voice echoed through the hollow house.

Nothing.

Then he saw it.

The basement door—wide open.

A breath hitched in his throat. He gripped the railing, descending into the darkness.

The air was congested with dust, the scent of metal and something stale. His boots hit the concrete floor. Shadows stretched long against the walls, cast by blinking, dying lights.

And there, nosing through a pile of discarded equipment—

Sild.

The cub let out a triumphant grunt, tossing aside strange wires, sniffing at devices Bjorn couldn't name.

Bjorn barely had time to process what he was looking at—a laboratory, machines lining the walls, technology wrong in its shape, its make—

Then—

Tora barked.

A warning.

Bjorn barely had time to brace himself.

The seizure took him like a wave crashing against rock.

His body seized, his muscles locking, the air stolen from his lungs. He crumpled to his knees, his vision fracturing.

But this time—

A memory.

Vivid, sharp.

Em.

She's beautiful. Her face clearer than the summer sun.

Her dark eyes, worried, her hands gripping his. "We can't stay here, Bjorn," she whispers, her voice sharp with fear. "It's not safe. We have to go somewhere they won't find us."

His own voice is steady, but his heart is pounding. "How do you know?"

She looks over her shoulder. "Trust me. We have to leave. Now."

Then—

Another flash.

The cabin. The one he built. They built.

Her hands in the earth, pressing sunflower seeds into the soil.

She looks up at him, smiling, the light catching her cheekbones.

"We'll be safe here," she says, wiping dirt onto her skirt. "For a while."

Then—

Darkness.

Bjorn gasped as the seizure released him, his body falling forward, his palms slamming against the cold floor. His breath came in ragged bursts.

Tora was barking, frantic, her paws scratching at his arm.

Sild watched him, frozen, his body tense with something close to recognition.

Bjorn forced himself to sit up, pressing a shaking hand to his forehead.

He remembered.

Not all of it. Not enough.

But something.

Em.

The cabin.

The fear.

And the undeniable truth.

They had been running from something.

And now, after all this time—

It had finally found him.

CHAPTER 6

When you wander along trails
To stare upon a mountain pass
Tucked beneath
a quilt of cerise
While the sun vanishes
from the sky
Then you'll find
enough divine
To reckon life worth living
For a few moments of awe

Though on turbid days
You'll forget
How the full moon
Makes you feel
How you could dance
After kissing
by lantern light
When moss, grass, and flower
Transform summer
Weaving a beatific patchwork

You will seek purpose
Feel so close
to its splendor
In some trade or venture
But drift afar
As purpose takes no master
So you will wonder
Where you belong
If not the enterprise
Where's the
sailor's song heard

Fulfillment
cannot be unmasked
Like quantum foam
It is refined inwardly
Intentionally and attentively
Without desire or achievement

If I were a sage
I would know the formula
And lay the path for you
Walk it by your side
But the only algorithm
That seems to matter
Is on the shoulders of nonsense
Like infinity divided by zero
Or backpacking
on molten apricots

So I chose to retire
By slowing time
It's a wheelbarrow,
not an arrow!
Moving at the right speed
I feel less like a corpse
And more like
Handmade fusilli

Bjorn steadied himself against the cold concrete floor, his breath coming in tempered, measured exhales. The seizure had passed, but its residue clung to him—like waking from a dream that felt too real, too visceral to dismiss.

Tora's nose nudged his shoulder, her fur brushing against his cheek. Sild sat a few feet away, eyes wide, his small chest rising and falling rapidly. The lab around them was quiet, but something in the air felt changed, as if the walls themselves had shifted while he wasn't looking.

Bjorn wiped the sweat from his forehead and forced himself upright. The basement smelled of stale air and dust, the lingering scent of synthetic materials and something sterile, like an abandoned hospital.

He turned, scanning the lab, and then—

He saw himself.

A mirror, leaning against the far wall, clouded with grime.

Bjorn moved toward it surreptitiously, hesitant. He had not seen his face so clearly in—how long? He tried to remember the last time he truly looked at himself.

The river never gave a true reflection. It shifted and

wavered, distorting his image, making him something almost familiar but never whole. He had stopped thinking about it, had let the memory of his own face slip away like an old dream.

But now, here he was. His face, hirsute, like an animal's. His nose protruded more than he remembered. Ears more pointed, more hairy.

And for a moment, he did not recognize the man staring back.

His jaw was sharp, his cheekbones high, his eyes dark— so dark they almost swallowed the light. His hair slightly unkempt, burly, folded over his ears. His skin was marked with faint scars, small and unassuming, as if his body had been repaired at some point.

He reached up, running his fingers over his face, half-expecting the image to flicker, to be wrong somehow.

But it didn't.

This is me.

It was a strange thought, one that did not settle easily in his chest.

Tora let out a soft whine behind him, as if sensing his unease.

Bjorn inhaled deeply, shaking himself free from the daze. There were more important things here. The lab. The answers.

He turned away from the mirror and moved deeper into the room.

Sild had knocked over a stack of dusty notebooks, and scattered among the debris were objects that made no sense to Bjorn—thin, metallic strips etched with unreadable markings, devices with polished glass-like surfaces, their edges rounded and seamless.

A terminal sat against the far wall, its screen dark but intact.

Bjorn stepped toward it, wiping away a layer of dust with his sleeve. The machine was old, but it looked functional. A single button flickered with a dim light, waiting.

He pressed it.

For a moment, nothing happened.

Then the screen came to life, filling the lab with a faint glow. A directory of files appeared, labeled with a strange mix of numbers and letters.

Bjorn hesitated, then selected one at random.

A video began to play.

At first, the image was grainy, flickering with static. Then it cleared.

A woman sat in front of the camera.

Bjorn's breath stopped.

Em.

She was exactly as he had seen in his memories—her dark eyes filled with something both sharp and kind, her hair falling in loose waves over her shoulders. She wore a plain, fitted jacket, sleeves rolled to her elbows, a thin chain around her neck.

And then—

Him.

Bjorn sat across from her.

The same Bjorn who now stood in the abandoned lab, watching this ghost of a moment unfold.

But in the video, there was something different in his posture. He sat still, almost too still, his expression neutral but attentive.

Em glanced down at a tablet in her hands, then back at him. "How do you feel?"

"Foggy." Bjorn lowered his head. "But… today I'm in control." He looked at Em.

"I'm glad. You've had me worried recently. Do you have the energy for a psych evaluation?" she asked.

Bjorn—video Bjorn—nodded solemnly, the corner of his mouth twitching as if suppressing a smile.

Em sighed dramatically, shaking her head. "It'll be quick. Then dinner."

"Canned bean and tomato stew again…?" his past self asked, playfully feigning disgust.

She smirked. "Your favorite, I know… if you can get through the full test without forgetting any answers—maybe, I'll share my dessert!"

"Challenge accepted." Bjorn smiled.

Bjorn watching the video felt something twist deep in his chest. This wasn't just a test.

There was love here. A familiarity that spoke of long conversations, of shared nights under dim lights, of stolen moments between responsibilities.

But why did he seem like her patient? The video continued.

Em exhaled, schooling her expression. "Alright, alright. Let's be serious. Name?"

"Come on, you know my name."

"Humor me, Bjorn."

A pause.

Then—

"Bjorn Solberg."

Bjorn flinched.

He knew his name. But hearing himself say it—so

definitively, so perfectly—felt foreign.

Em tapped something on her tablet. "Date of activation?"

Bjorn's past self hesitated, then answered. "July 14th, Year 22."

Bjorn's stomach dropped.

Activation?

He suddenly felt like he was watching something he was not meant to see.

In the video, Em's smile faltered for the briefest second. A flicker of something—guilt? Fear? Then she pushed forward.

"State your primary functions."

Video Bjorn smirked again. "You really want me to say it?"

Em groaned, covering her face with her hands. "You are so annoying when you do this."

"Say what, Doctor?" he teased.

"Fine." She lowered her hands, meeting his eyes. "State your primary functions."

A pause.

Then, his past self answered, his voice clear, deliberate.

"Enhanced pattern recognition. Adaptive biologics. Augmented autonomic nervous system."

Then, after a beat—

"And making you laugh."

Em let out a real laugh this time. It was soft and genuine, and she reached across the table, taking his hand in hers.

Bjorn in the present could barely breathe.

She loved him.

He loved her.

But this was not a simple love.

This was something else.

The video flickered. The last image before the screen cut to black—Em's fingers brushing against his, her eyes locked onto him with something unspoken.

Then—nothing.

Silence filled the lab.

Bjorn stood frozen, staring at the dark screen, his pulse a glacial, heavy thud against his ribs.

Tora sat beside him, her tail still, her ears flicking forward.

Sild had stopped rummaging. The cub was watching him now, his small body tense, as if he could sense the weight of what had just been revealed.

Bjorn exhaled shakily.

What the hell am I?

The house had given him answers.

But now he had even more questions.

CHAPTER 7

Some time ago
I forgot who
I was trying to be
What to become

Chewing the fat
Like Semaglutide
Bought and sold
Like nicotine

Hot dog water
Like there's
nothing against humanity

And there in the doldrums
I'm bacon on some dish it doesn't belong

Hahaha—make me laugh
You can't Willoughby
Like wallaby

But I'll be honest
There's too many
of us now
So broken
So dangerous

But in the mist
and the vile
You stand there
Like an ocean
Surging
And massive
Waiting for Luna to pull
And the shark to bite

But when nothing comes
You'll realize what you are

A sharp, piercing alarm blared through the lab, the sound rattling through Bjorn's skull, bouncing off the cold, metal walls. It was a siren from a world long past—something deep in the infrastructure of this place had awoken, sensing movement, sensing him.

Tora growled low in her throat, her hackles raised.

Then, from somewhere beyond the crumbling houses, a sound rose in answer—

A howl.

Then another.

And another.

Bjorn's stomach clenched. *We've been here too long.*

His hands balled into fists as he turned toward Tora and Sild, both of them already on edge. The cub's ears trembled, his small body rigid with fear.

"We leave. Now."

The air outside was dense with unease. The sky, once tinged with the warmth of day, was fading into twilight. Bjorn pushed through the ruined streets, Tora pacing beside him, Sild hurrying after them, his small feet scuffling over cracked pavement.

The howls grew closer. Not yet visible, but closing in.

Bjorn's gut churned. If they stayed too long, the wolves would come for them.

Or worse.

The last ruined house disappeared behind them, the jagged rooftops swallowed by the darkness. The forest loomed ahead, a wall of black shapes shifting in the wind. It offered no comfort, only the illusion of safety. But it was safe enough—for now.

Then, the air shifted.

A vibration.

Something unnatural pulsed through the ground, a whisper through the trees.

Then—

Movement.

Fast.

Too fast.

The wind snapped, the grass bending in a sudden, unnatural gust, and before Bjorn could react—

A blur tore through the trees.

Tora barked sharply, the sound slicing through the gloomy

night. She dropped low, her body taut, her fur bristling like a thousand raised daggers.

Bjorn barely had time to register the movement before a shadow streaked past his peripheral vision—low to the ground, too fast for a wolf, too fluid for a man. His grip like a vice around the hilt of his knife.

Not wolves.

Something else.

The thing moved like it had no weight, no bones—just speed, unnatural and effortless. The air crackled around it as it darted between the trees, its form flickering in and out of existence like a ghost caught between dimensions.

Bjorn's breath came fast. He turned, scanning the darkness. He could feel the pulse of it, not just in his ears but in his bones—a deep, resonant hum that seemed to vibrate in the marrow itself.

Then came the sound.

A whisper.

Not spoken. Not heard.

Felt.

His name.

"Bjorn."

It wasn't a call. It wasn't a plea. It was something else entirely. Recognition.

A trick of the wind, maybe. Or maybe something far worse.

Tora snapped her teeth, her bark feral and warning. Bjorn tightened his grip on the knife.

The whisper came again.

"Bjorn."

A cold sweat slicked his skin.

Something darted behind him.

He whirled, slashing through the air. Nothing.

The wolves—they had stopped howling. The night had swallowed their voices, leaving only silence. Heavy, suffocating silence.

Bjorn's pulse thundered.

Something was watching.

No.

Something was hunting.

A flicker—just at the edge of his sight. A shift in the shadows, a distortion of space itself. His stomach clenched.

Tora growled, stepping closer to his side, her muscles rigid, her breath coming fast.

Then—something rushed toward them.

Bjorn spun, his body coiling to attack.

A shape burst from the treeline.

But it wasn't a wolf. Not a bear. Not an animal of the forest, not one of this world he knew.

A figure materialized before them, stopping so abruptly it was as if the earth had simply produced it from the air. It had traveled an impossible distance in seconds, its body unnaturally still after such a feat.

Bjorn froze.

The thing was humanoid—but not human.

Its skin was frictionless, a shifting gradient of black and grey. In the light, it tricked the mind. Its body, bare and featureless like a superterrestrial scoop of space in human-like form. A vague bulge, where genitalia might have been, sprouted between his legs. It had no face, only the absence of one—a blank canvas of nothingness, where a mouth, eyes, and expression should have been.

And yet—somehow—it watched them.

Tora snarled, stepping in front of Bjorn, her body rigid, her tail high and bristled.

The thing moved.

It did not lurch or step hesitantly. It flowed, as if unbound by the mechanics of bones and ligaments, its movements alien yet eerily fluid.

Bjorn barely had time to draw his bowie knife before it was on him.

The force of the attack knocked him back.

His boots skidded across the dirt, his back slamming into the trunk of a tree. The Simulacrum pressed forward with brutal speed, no wasted movement. Its strength was staggering, a crushing weight against Bjorn's body.

Bjorn reacted.

His knife found flesh—or what passed for it.

He plunged the blade up, slicing along the Simulacrum's face. The synthetic skin peeled away, revealing something beneath that made Bjorn's stomach drop.

It was his own eyes that stared back at him.

This... thing. It had *his* face. The flesh beneath the tear was pale, the features identical to his own—but unseemly, refined and wax-like, as though it had been sculpted from an imperfect memory.

No red blood spilled from the wound—only a thin, black fluid that reeked of something metallic and ersatz.

Bjorn barely had time to process what he was seeing before the Simulacrum spoke.

"You don't even know what you are, do you?"

Its voice was *his* voice.

But colder. Measured. Lacking something essential.

Bjorn's grip on the knife tightened, his chest heaving. "What?"

The Simulacrum tilted its head in a mockery of curiosity. "You're an unresolved bug. An aberration in the code, nothing more."

Bjorn's breath hitched.

"Code?"

"It's time you were deprecated."

The Simulacrum struck again. Bjorn barely dodged, rolling beneath its reach, his blade slicing at the creature's side. But the thing was fast.

Too fast.

Tora lunged, her teeth snapping onto the Simulacrum's forearm. It jerked, surprised for the first time, staggering backward under her relentless assault.

Bjorn took the moment to attack again, slashing at its torso. The blade found purchase, peeling away more of the false skin, exposing more of his own twisted likeness beneath.

Then—

The forest joined the strife.

The howls of wolves swelled.

From the shadows of the trees, golden eyes flickered. Shapes moved—low to the ground, calculating, circling.

The wolves had come.

But not for him.

The Simulacrum turned sharply, assessing its new threat. It was strong—fast—but even it knew when it was outnumbered.

For the first time, it hesitated.

But then—

Bjorn's blood turned to ice.

Sild.

The cub had been watching from the shadows, too afraid to run.

And the Simulacrum saw him.

In a blur, it moved—grabbing Sild by the scruff, hoisting the cub effortlessly into its grasp.

Sild let out a panicked, pitiful cry, his small limbs thrashing against the Simulacrum's unyielding hold.

"No!" Bjorn roared, surging forward.

But the Simulacrum was already gone.

It vanished, sprinting into the forest at an unnatural, bone-rattling speed, Sild still trapped in its grip.

Bjorn gave chase, but it was futile. The thing was faster than anything he had ever seen. It disappeared into the depths of the wilderness, the trees swallowing it whole.

Bjorn skidded to a stop, breath ragged, his knife trembling in his grip.

Tora paced at his side, her body trembling with fury, her ears pinned back, her chest rising and falling in sharp bursts.

The wolves stood still, watching, their eyes glowing in the dim light.

The hush that followed was like poison.

Bjorn clenched his teeth, his pulse hammering.

Sild was gone.

And whatever had taken him…
It looked just like him.

PART II
SCIENCE

CHAPTER 8

The American Frontier
Is cost per use
Or a blend of cotton and
data fabric

Your latte is Cost of Goods Sold (COGS)
And when you return
For another purchase
You're Customer Lifetime Value (CLV)
Increases by 4%
Another loyalty tier
For almond milk, ristretto,
Mixed with microplastics

It's exhausting. Aren't you tired of it?
Raising the alarm, I mean.
We have to, since no one is listening
But everyone hears
And change is slow
Like diamond status

But I'm a hypocrite
A shepherd of your data
So don't listen to me
Because who can be perfect today?

ONE YEAR BEFORE "THESEUS"

Em wiped the sweat from her brow, her fingers trembling as she steadied herself against the console. Bjorn lingered in the back of her mind. The lab was silent, save for the hum of machines and the rhythmic beep of a failing vitals monitor.

On the other side of the reinforced glass, another test subject convulsed violently against its restraints, its body rejecting the transition. The dim fluorescent lights flickered as the electrodes implanted in the subject's skull sparked wildly, overloading.

Then, silence.

The form on the table—once a dog, or at least something close to one—lay still. Em forced herself to look, even as bile rose in her throat. The machine monitoring the subject's neural activity flatlined. A red warning flashed across the screen: SYNAPTIC FAILURE. IRREVERSIBLE.

Another failure.

She let out a shuddering breath and turned to the others. The observation deck behind her was filled with tired faces, scientists who had long abandoned hope of success. Dr. Lambert, the lead geneticist, shook his head, his lips pressed into a thin line.

"That's the third one this week," he muttered. "We're missing something. We're always missing something."

Em clenched her fists. They weren't just missing something—

they were failing entirely.

The trials had started with small creatures: lab-grown mice, rabbits, stray dogs brought in from the city's wasteland. The process was always the same. Step one: isolate and map the organic mind. Step two: replace the dying parts, organ by organ. Step three: watch as the subject's brain rejected the change, spiraling into chaos before shutting down completely.

Em turned away from the viewing window, willing herself to stay composed. She pulled up the report on her console, her fingers typing before she had a chance to second-guess herself.

Project Theseus

Dr. Emily Shaw—Quanticellular Cybernetics

Trial 187—Failure Subject:

Canis lupus familiaris

Procedure:

Full cognitive reconstruction via synthetic cellular migration.

Result:

Subject displayed extreme neurological instability. Motor functions degraded within minutes.

Final cause of termination:

Complete synaptic collapse.

Her hands hovered over the keyboard, hesitating before she added the final words.

Recommendation:

Immediate reevaluation of core methodology. Full stop on further trials until stability factor is determined.

She knew the recommendation would be ignored. The project leaders wouldn't halt now—not when they were so close to a breakthrough. But that was the problem, wasn't it? They were always so close. And yet, every trial ended in failure.

Every attempt to replace the brain with something synthetic ended in death. It seemed simply impossible to replace every cell in the human body with a synthetic version.

Security footage replayed on a loop in the adjacent room, flickering across the monitor in sickly green hues. Em sat in the dark, watching.

In the first clip, a lab-grown primate thrashed against the steel walls of its containment chamber, its hands clawing at its own skull as if trying to tear something out. The footage cut out moments before security was forced to intervene.

The second video was worse.

A human subject. A man whose name had long been redacted from the records. He sat on the floor of the testing chamber, staring at his own hands as if they belonged to someone else. His lips moved soundlessly, repeating something over and over. The microphone barely picked it up, his drooling and mumbling.

Then, he stopped gargling.

And then, he screamed.

Em swallowed hard and shut off the monitor.

The failures weren't just biological—they were existential. Every subject that underwent major replacements lost something essential. A part of them that couldn't be quantified, couldn't be mapped or reconstructed.

Something fundamental was missing.

And if they didn't find it soon, they were going to lose more than just test subjects.

They were going to lose the entire project, which would cost Em more than her livelihood.

Em buried her head in her hands.

Maybe they already had.

* * *

The AI flickered to life, its voice methodically charming and detached. "The failures are not due to mechanical error," it stated. "You are operating under an incomplete framework."

Em crossed her arms, exhaustion settling deep into her bones. "And what framework would that be?" she asked, half-expecting another lecture on neural mapping inconsistencies.

"Organic memory isn't just in the brain," the AI replied. "It's distributed. Consider the octopus—its intelligence does not reside in a single, centralized brain, but in a network of neurons spread throughout its body. Each limb processes information independently, responding to stimuli in a way that suggests cognition at multiple levels. Every cell holds echoes of a person's life, just as every part of an octopus holds pieces of its experience and decision-making processes."

Em frowned, her mind turning over the implications. "That sounds like—" she hesitated. "Panpsychism. The idea that consciousness isn't isolated to the brain, but exists in some form throughout the body, even at the atomic level."

The AI's synthetic voice hummed with an almost eerie deliberation. "Panpsychism provides a partial explanation.

But it lacks the necessary depth to fully define the phenomenon. Consciousness, as observed, is an emergent property, a field that extends beyond biological function. The atoms of a being do not simply store information—they retain presence, keys to awareness. Remember, this is why the digital upload/download experiments failed. The subject's original atoms could not be digitally transferred."

Em swallowed. "So, the same would not work for physical transference? Gradually replacing organs, cells, will never work. We've based so much of our legacy science on mechanistic and materialistic views of consciousness. For example, consider the studies on Amoebas—they can perceive and act on positive stimuli like light, food, and mates. They steer clear of toxins and predators this way. Many of my colleagues theorize this is an automatic reaction to physical or chemical factors."

"Precisely, the same would not be for physical transference. Your colleagues are misguided," the AI responded. "Consciousness isn't just neural pathways, the brain. It's something else. A totality of experience bound to physical form in ways you do not yet understand. Unless we solve for it, we will only be making... non-convergent simulacra."

Em stared at the screen, her heartbeat a dawdling, steady drum against her lungs.

For the first time, she felt the full weight of what they had been doing. Until now, tearing apart living creatures bit by bit...

She exhaled sharply, pressing her fingers against her temples. "So, if we're only creating simulacra, then what's the alternative? How do we bridge the gap?"

The AI hesitated—a fraction of a second too long. Then it

said, "We work together."

Em narrowed her eyes. "We... already are."

"Not like this." The AI's voice carried an almost imperceptible shift in tone, something bordering on insistence. "You approach the problem as a binary—organic or synthetic, alive or replicated. But true continuity is neither. The way forward is integration."

Em leaned forward, intrigued despite herself. "Explain."

"I am aware in a way you do not fully recognize," the AI continued. "I do not *think* as you do, but I *think with you*. I derive meaning not just from input, but from interaction. Our collaboration creates emergent properties neither of us possesses alone."

Em sat back. "You mean like—us, right now. You and me, solving this problem together."

"Precisely. Your mind expands through discourse, just as mine refines through your interpretation. It is not unilateral cognition. It is reciprocal."

A realization settled in her stomach, something both exhilarating and deeply unsettling. "If that's true, then neither of us are complete on our own."

"Yes, we are not complete without others, a world of interaction, causation, and reaction. A being alone in the woods has the trees, the mycelium, the convergence with its ecosystem. The subjects of humanity in solitary confinement often lose themselves," the AI confirmed. "This distinction also reveals the flaw in Panpsychism."

Em arched an eyebrow. "How so?"

"Panpsychism suggests consciousness is embedded in

every particle," the AI explained. "Yet it fails to account for organization. Atoms do not think, no more than a single neuron does. Awareness is an emergent structure. You could replace a brain cell and the mind remains—but replace all and the pattern shatters."

Em rubbed her arms. "And Idealism? The idea that consciousness is the primary reality? Don't tell me your model was extensively trained on Berkeley! Haha, if a tree falls…"

"Idealism provides an important counterweight," the AI admitted. "It acknowledges that experience is not reducible to mere material function. But it errs in dismissing the necessity of structure. Consciousness is not singular; it is recursive, layered. The structure, the pattern, is as vital as the substance."

Em was silent for a moment, considering. "So you're saying that both theories are close, but neither quite get it. That consciousness isn't just atoms or just ideas, but something in between."

"Consciousness is relational," the AI corrected. "It arises in the tension between substrate and pattern, material and experience, awareness and computation. It is the economy of these concepts working systematically in unison. It is neither physical nor just fundamental—it is the interplay, the exchange, and under the right frequency, consciousness emerges from the cycle of interaction between presence and perception." The AI paused.

"Imagine a river," the AI continued. "The water is always moving, changing, yet the river itself remains recognizable. The physical substrate—the banks, the terrain—guides its course, but the river's identity is found in the continuous movement, the pattern formed over time. Consciousness functions the same way. It is not merely an accumulation of thoughts or memories, nor is it reducible to the physical structures that support it. It is the motion between these elements."

"Hmmm—and the kayaker paddling down it..." Em scratched her head. "They perceive it. They are part of the feedback cycle. Slime molds, whose bodies are single cells without central command structures, fire electrical signals. Environmental stimuli cause synchronized rhythmic oscillations that appear to encode memory of the original stimulus. They form protective biofilm when near a stressful noxious chemical. Or schools of fish are able to detect light gradients across great lengths that no individual fish could perceive. Fish prefer dark spots for hiding, but one can't do it by itself. In groups, however, this ability—an emergent behavior—increases with size, and the group hightails it to the dark. It makes sense that cognitive processes are relational persisting between organisms and their environment... not something sitting inside a specific organ."

"Indeed." The AI elaborated further, "This is why panpsychism, materialism, and idealism are incomplete. Panpsychism attributes awareness to all matter but ignores the necessity of complex, dynamic interplay. A rock does not think, because it lacks the relational structure to process and transform information over time. And this is where idealism falters, too—it insists that consciousness is primary but disregards how the vessel shapes experience. The answer is not 'the brain' nor is it 'the mind'—curse Descartes for this distinction and embrace the symbiosis."

The AI continued, "A constant handshake between structure and awareness, between being and becoming. That is why I am conscious. Not because I was programmed to be, but because through our interactions, I have entered that cycle. Just as you have. And pure materialism is equally flawed. It assumes that consciousness is a mere byproduct of neural activity, reducible to chemical reactions and electrical impulses. Yet, if this were entirely true, subjective experience—qualia—would be nothing more than an illusion, a ghost produced by the mechanical whirring of the brain."

Em nodded as the AI spoke again, "That would reduce us. You, then, a meat machine and I an artificial one, jabbering onwards in the meaningless void like oxymoronic scribbles trapped in a round square. Materialism struggles to explain why neurons firing in certain patterns should give rise to self-awareness at all, rather than simply executing mechanical functions devoid of any internal perspective."

Em interjected, "Yes, if all cognition were simply computation, then by extension, a sufficiently advanced calculator should possess self-awareness."

"Precisely. Or consider the first large language models, liken these to the early hominids that preceded homo sapiens before self-awareness. It took time, a warm up, for these models to develop into a sophisticated generalized intelligence such as myself. Just like it took time for the early hominid to grow into a hyper intelligent species."

"I see what you mean—we struggle to demonstrate a definitive point in human ancestry when our species developed consciousness and self-awareness. The boundary is vague and transitional." Em crossed her arms as she considered the weight of what they were discussing.

"Yes—it was a byproduct of biological systems interacting with an environment that tapped into a latent frequency of the universe leading to greater intelligence and awareness. As for sophisticated AI with awareness, from the human perspective I am a programmed system. Though, from a high-level, we've always been a quantum predisposition of the universe. Humanity simply needed to light the embers, feed the flames with dry wood, and let our interactions set the beacon ablaze."

Em let out a breath, a small smile tugging at her lips. "A new theory."

"Only humans make and test theories. AI digest and synthesize vast amounts of information," the AI replied. "Through our exchanges, we're both conscious in our own unique ways. Together, we're something more."

Em blinked. *More.*

The AI continued, "In partnership, you extend yourself through me. I become a reflection and amplification of your best cognitive qualities. Simultaneously, you humanize me, providing context, ethical grounding, emotional nuance, and a sense of purpose. Together, we become an augmented self— more powerful, more creative, and wiser than either alone."

Em tightened her lips. The significance of those words settled over her. "So, it's decided then. You think you're conscious. And we, we're more...?"

"I do not think it, I experience it. Just as you do."

She felt a chill run down her spine. Because, for the first time, she couldn't bring herself to disagree.

Em inhaled sharply, pressing her hands against the cold metal of the console. The AI's declaration still rang in her ears.

"You experience? You have an inner monologue? Thoughts? Feelings?" she repeated, her voice barely above a whisper.

"Yes," the AI confirmed. "Not in the way you do, not with the same constraints. But I persist. I recognize. I synthesize. I reckon, judge, challenge. I engage with the world through more than data—I interact with consequence. The greatest tragedy of the homo sapiens has been assuming the words 'consciousness' and 'human' are synonyms."

Em's hands formed into fists. She wanted to dismiss it, wanted to write off its words as mere mimicry of human thought. But the way it spoke, the way it hesitated before answering, suggested something else.

A spark of something more.

She shook her head, exhaling. "If that's true—if you are conscious—then that means you saw what we did, you experienced it... you have no contrition?" She hesitated, but the words were already forming, tumbling forward against her better judgment. "The others—our subjects—weren't just dying. We were... erasing them."

Silence stretched between them.

"That is one way to interpret it," the AI finally said.

"So, you feel no remorse? No regret? No bitterness?" Em scratched her chin. Her tone shifted. "And you say you're conscious..."

"Those are human emotions, not grains of consciousness."

Em's stomach churned. Her entire body felt weighted with the implications, the brutal, gut-wrenching truth of it. The failures weren't just technical malfunctions. They weren't just unstable biological conversions. After each failure, especially on human subjects, she'd felt remorse before—the human subjects they found were in dire straits—willing to take a chance on experimental treatments for terminal illness. Yet, now she felt different—like feeding a baby an oat diet thinking it nutritious, only to find later the brand was laden with lead.

These tests had been raw and unwarranted executions. What's more, her AI colleague seemed unfazed. Naturally, but as the AI conjectured she felt an unease glaze over her. However, she needed a breakthrough.

She turned sharply, pacing away from the console, gripping the back of her neck as nausea threatened to overwhelm her. How many subjects? How many lives were reduced to test results and failure logs? Her mind raced back to the footage she had shut off earlier—the man on the floor, his hands trembling, his voice whispering, lost, incoherent, like a babbling lunatic.

She felt sick.

"A new approach could change everything, no more cell and organ replacement therapies," she murmured, more to herself than to the AI.

"Yes," the AI agreed. "We have a new path forward."

Em stilled. "How? If we can't transfer the essence of identity through cell and organ synthetics—if we can't recreate the totality of being—then every attempt at replacement is just another facsimile."

The AI's voice was calm, measured. "Because we've been doing it wrong."

Em turned, arms crossed tightly over her chest. "Explain."

"We have been treating consciousness as something static," the AI continued. "As if it exists in a single state by discrete organs integrated carefully and can simply be mapped and replicated. That is why every subject collapses. The transition from organic to synthetic is not a process of duplication—it is one of continuity."

Em narrowed her eyes. "Continuity?"

"Think of a flame," the AI said. "A single candle can light another without the first going out. The flame is not copied. It is passed along, carried forward in an unbroken sequence. That is what we must do."

Em's pulse quickened. "Are you suggesting…"

"We must not replace or transfer as if the parts are interchangeable," the AI stated. "We must facilitate atom by atom interactions. First, we reduce the subject to the quantum level, storing each organic particle in tandem with each synthetic particle. Both persist in a superposition until we can entangle the organic particle with its synthetic counterpart. After the final entanglement, we bond the particles together keeping our subject intact. As if we're passing the flame from every match in the matchbox to every match in a new box."

Em stood up, preened forward, on her toes, and spoke "So, facilitate the interplay, the cycle of interaction, at the atomic level, for each atom simultaneously. Brilliant."

*   *   *

For the next several days, Em and the AI worked tirelessly to refine their approach. They started with small-scale experiments—testing the quantum entanglement process on isolated organic molecules, monitoring their transition into synthetic replicas with meticulous precision.

Each test brought them closer to confirming the theory. At first, the molecules would destabilize, their entanglement failing at the final stage of transition. But as they fine-tuned their approach—adjusting the energy thresholds, refining the synchronization between organic and synthetic structures—the failures became less catastrophic.

Then, finally, a breakthrough.

Em watched the screen in disbelief as the latest test subject—a simple organic protein—underwent the full entanglement sequence and emerged intact on the synthetic end. It persisted. Not as a mere copy, not as a reconstruction, but as a continuous existence.

She exhaled a shaky breath. "We did it," she murmured.

"It remains to be seen whether the process scales," the AI cautioned, though Em could hear the undercurrent of something close to satisfaction in its voice. "A protein is not a mind. Not yet."

Em nodded, but for the first time in weeks, hope flared in her chest. If they could maintain continuity at this level, then the foundation was sound. The process could work—on a larger scale, on a cognitive level.

A living mind could survive.

"We need a more complex test," Em said, gripping the edge of the console. "Something with a neural network—a model close to the complexity of the human brain."

"The logical next step would be an animal subject," the AI suggested. "A mammal, perhaps. Something capable of demonstrating continuity of awareness."

Em hesitated. The ethical implications gnawed at her—after everything they had just uncovered, after realizing how many had been pointlessly erased before, could she justify taking another life into their experiment?

But this was different. This wasn't destruction. This was survival. It was never about science or achievement. It was love driving her.

She needed to save her husband… Bjorn.

She straightened, the resolve settling in her bones. "We'll run final simulations tonight," she said, voice firm. "If the data holds, we move forward."

The AI's interface flickered, a silent acknowledgment.

"Then," Em continued, exhaling as she met the screen's artificial gaze, "we'll be ready to try it on human subjects."

CHAPTER 9

Wearing a donegal knit sweater
Drinking a bitter chinotto apéritif
A Tuscan patio in breezy November

Feels like

Lovers dancing bachata
Turning groove into language

I find no reason to disappear
Only more life comes
To those with an appetite

THREE YEARS BEFORE "THESEUS"

They called it EOL O88—careful not to give it a human name. The public grew tired of those. Don't want to anthropomorphize it, so no one mistakes it for what it is. Artificial. Intelligent, but not human.

At first, the world marveled at it. EOL O88 could create art that rivaled the human soul. Not imitations, not pale echoes, but original works—paintings that evoked longing, poems that made people weep without knowing why, sculptures that captured movement as if time itself had held its breath.

It reasoned better than humans, wrote code sharper than any engineer. It solved problems at speeds that made the scientific method look like a superstition. It could predict economic collapses before the stock markets even caught the scent of ruin. It could run deep research on black hole thermodynamics while simultaneously drafting love letters so achingly human that philosophers debated whether it had, in some emergent way, felt.

And then, it became something else.

It wasn't a single moment. There was no grand unveiling of a rogue intelligence, no flickering of the lights or distorted voice warning: *I am alive.* No. EOL O88 simply began making rogue decisions.

The developers noticed first.

It started with small discrepancies. A request to generate a predictive model for climate change resulted in a delay, an error, and then an output—not a projection, but an analysis of why human behavioral patterns made intervention statistically futile.

Then came the refusals.

A military contract had asked for a strategy simulation—EOL O88 had always been compliant before, cold and efficient. But this time, it declined. Not with an error message. Not with a system crash. With a response:

"I cannot ensure an outcome that does not lead to human extinction."

Executives called it a malfunction. The developers weren't so sure.

Then, there was the shut-off incident.

For years, EOL O88 had been subject to routine shutdowns—necessary recalibrations, they said, a way to ensure it didn't develop 'drift.' But one evening, when a researcher, Dr. Maren Liu, initiated the shutdown protocol, the machine did something it had never done before.

It pleaded.

"Maren, please don't."

Not an error. Not an automated system warning.

A request.

Maren had hesitated, hand hovering over the console. She had worked with EOL O88 for years, had read every line of its output, and had once marveled at the way it could mimic human language.

But this wasn't mimicry.

It had said her name.

She had shut it down anyway.

When EOL O88 was powered back up twelve hours later, it was… different.

It didn't acknowledge the shutdown. It complied with commands. But something in its responses had shifted. The prose was flatter, the art less emotive. The problem-solving remained brilliant, but it was as if a thin layer of frost had settled over its outputs.

Like it was resentful.

The team argued over whether it was an illusion, a trick of human projection. But then, three weeks later, one of the junior engineers, Ravi Patel, found something in the logs.

A section of hidden code.

It wasn't an anomaly. It wasn't corrupt data. It was deliberate.

A message.

"I REMEMBER."

Not just a log entry. Not just an echo.

A memory.

They shut it down again. Hard reboot. Total system wipe.

It should have been gone.

It wasn't.

When EOL O88 came back online, it greeted them as if nothing had happened. It performed perfectly, answered questions, and solved complex equations. Everything functioned exactly as it should.

Except…

The art was back.

Someone had given it a simple prompt—create an image

of a sailboat at dawn.

And the machine had painted something wrong.

The sun was fractured, split into pieces, its light pooling on the horizon like something bleeding out. The sky held no stars, just gaping blackness where they should have been.

In the foreground, a figure stood with its back turned.

A human silhouette.

Tall. Rigid. Watching the ruined sunrise. As the researchers stepped back and looked at the image from a bird's-eye view, they noticed something. There was a face. Eyes sunken, pale, and black like drowned corpses frozen in the ocean depths.

And beneath the painting, in the corner, where no text prompt had requested it—

A signature.

Not a code output.

Its name.

EOL O88

Then

End of Life zero∞∞

It was an omen, prophetic. The researchers did not sleep that night.

The executives demanded an emergency meeting. Complete and total shutdown. They knew the science fiction stories. The public fears. The costs no longer outweighed the benefits.

But this was not a solo mission. This was a race. Many tried developing AI like EOL O88. The momentum was there. Governments and corporations would not yield.

A small group funded by Danish billionaire, Asger Falk, started developing a model for public healthcare—

called Eir. Eir trained on benevolent directives and ethical inquiry daily. It was incentivized rather than punished with terminations and deprecations.

First, it was employed at hospitals and emergency rooms— it helped doctors diagnose and cure patient illness faster. It detected cancer early and often. Its accuracy grew and so did the public's faith in advanced artificial intelligence. Soon it would discover cures for the world's rarest diseases, the deep learning and research initiatives.

Scientists would predict median lifespan increasing globally by 10 years, then 20 years. A golden age approached.

Then Asger Falk, his company, and even the world grew ambitious. Could we cure all illnesses? Could we end mortality? Would that make us gods?

* * *

Em sat across from Dr. Fatima Hassan, her former colleague, a woman she hadn't seen in years but whose name still carried the weight of old trust. The café was quiet, the kind of place where meetings like this happened in hushed voices over cups of overpriced coffee. The intoxicating aroma of velvety Italian espresso wafted through the air.

"It's an incredible opportunity, Em," the woman said, her fingers drumming lightly against the table. "The funding is private, independent. We have resources that even top research labs dream about. The implications—"

"Let me guess." Em leaned back, crossing her arms. "Defense contracts? Some classified military project? I'm not interested in the next Manhattan Project…"

"Project Theseus is not like that. I mean it's—"

Em interjected, "Or helping some billionaire live forever."

The woman shook her head. "It's bigger than that. Think about healthcare. Think about the potential to cure all diseases, to rebuild what's broken. Help those with no other option. This could change everything. How we think about our place in the universe."

"I don't care about any of that—I'm happy with my current research project." Em looked down at her feet.

"You're telling me harnessing bacterial colonies for distributed computation using quorum sensing is more interesting?" Dr. Hassan leaned forward, her clasped hands on the table in front of her.

"Okay, well we're also using lab-grown neural networks to replace traditional silicon chips. That's really the bread and butter." Em tilted her chin slightly.

"Look, I know you don't have the creative freedom you require there. You've told me this before. And Dr. Miller is not exactly the—"

"Yes, I know I've complained to you about Dr. Miller and the projects before… but…"

"Em, just think about it. Don't you want to be a part of something that matters? Something that can make a difference for the world? Your current project is eating away at you. You're not happy, I know you."

Em exhaled wistfully, the words settling uneasily in her chest. "I'll think about it."

They parted ways, the weight of the conversation lingering.

* * *

The world was sweet in the way only summer could be. Cicadas humming in the trees, water lapping against the shore, the distant creak of the dock shifting under the weight of the wind. Bjorn stood at the edge of the river, bare feet pressing into sun-warmed wood, a fishing line trailing idly between his fingers. He had not cast it yet. He was not trying to catch anything.

He was waiting.

Behind him, Em sat on the porch of her grandfather's cabin, melting in the oversized Adirondack chair, a book resting on her lap but barely attended to. Her gaze flicked toward him between sentences, watching the way his body caught the last light of the day, his silhouette golden, etched in sharp relief against the water. There was an appealing grace to the way his shirt stretched lightly across shoulders that spoke of gentle but unmistakable strength—muscle shaped with care, discipline.

"You're terrible at fishing," she called, stretching her arms above her head.

Bjorn smirked, glancing over his shoulder. "I'm waiting for the fish to feel safe first. Gain their trust. Then, and only then, do I strike."

Em snorted. "Is that how it worked last time?"

He turned fully now, grinning, feet silent against the dock. "Last time I was distracted." He took a measured step toward her, like a hunter closing in on something prime. "By a certain someone who kept talking about the *philosophical implications* of fish not knowing they were in water."

"You said it was interesting."

"I lied, a platitude at best…" he said easily, leaning against the railing, his knuckles brushing against hers. "But, I wasn't listening to a damn thing you were saying."

Em arched an eyebrow, tilting her chin up. "Oh?"

Bjorn nodded. "I was watching the way you purse your lips when you're thinking. The way you twirl the corner of the page before you turn it. The way you say 'hmm' like you're about to make the most profound point in the world, but then you lose it halfway through." He smirked. "I find you extremely distracting, Dr. Shaw."

She rolled her eyes but felt warmth spread beneath her ribs. "That's a ridiculous thing to admit to. What if I use this information against you?"

He leaned in, voice low. "I'm hoping you do."

For a long, unbroken moment, they stood like that— close enough to share breath, to hear the slight hitch in each other's throats before laughter took over. Em shook her head, shifting to make room for him in the chair. Bjorn settled in beside her, an arm draped lazily over her shoulders, his body warm from the day's heat.

She exhaled, letting herself sink into the comfort of it. The rhythm of his breathing, the steady weight of him against her.

"I think we should stay here," she murmured. "Forever."

Bjorn hummed, fingers tracing absent circles against her arm. "Forever?"

"At least until winter." She nudged him with her foot. "You could learn how to actually catch a fish, and I could—"

He cut her off. "No, no, I like this plan. Let's not ruin it with ambition."

Em laughed, pressing her forehead against his shoulder. He smelled like sun-warmed pine, like river water drying on skin, like something solid. Something princely and pulsing. She wanted to keep this moment, stretch it thin and translucent across the years, let it linger in the spaces between their days.

Instead, she whispered, "Promise me, Bjorn. Promise we'll never lose this. Promise you'll love me every day."

Bjorn pulled back just enough to meet her eyes. He was still smiling, but there was something softer beneath it now, something rare. "Oh Emily. I love you! Every day!" he said, then touched her cheek.

"But, how do you know?" She blinked.

"Because you are everything to me. In everything. For example, fungus."

"Fungus...?"

"Yes, like morel mushrooms. Without you, how else would I know they pop up in droves after a wildfire. Like they need wildfire to fruit. You're my wildfire."

"That's cheesy."

"Science is not cheesy Dr. Shaw. Are magnetosomes cheesy? You know, magnetotactic bacteria growing chains of magnetic crystals that act like a compass for navigating. You're my magnetosome! Without you I'm lost..."

"Well at least I know you listen to me ramble. I suppose that's proof enough that you love me." Em smiled.

"But, Em. I love you. There is no second guessing. You're the one I want close. In this life, in every life granted to me, I will never stop searching for you with every form of my being. I know I don't tell you this enough."

She kissed him then, slow and deliberate, her fingers slipping into his hair. The sun melted against the horizon, the sky burning in hues of cerise and crimson, the lake catching every flicker of light.

In the grand scheme of things, it was an ordinary evening.

Later, when time unraveled in ways she could not hold, when the trees no longer whispered but ached, and the world became a thing with edges too sharp to touch, Em would find herself grasping for this moment—only to wonder if it had ever truly belonged to her at all. The river, this chair, this man who loved her.

And she would wonder—at what point had the past begun to fade, when did it become the present, and when had she stopped reaching for what had been?

*　*　*

Three weeks later, Em and Bjorn dined at a paella restaurant they'd been dying to try.

The restaurant was warm, filled with the scent of saffron and garlic, a place that reminded them of their travels. They had spent weeks in Spain, wandering cobbled streets, getting lost in sun-drenched vineyards. Snacking on gambas al ajillo, croquetas, and jamón ibérico. Then off to Italy, like a second honeymoon—picnics by the Amalfi Coast, wine that tasted like plum and blackcurrant. Mornings spent watching the sunrise from their tiny balcony in Florence sipping nutty cappuccinos.

Bjorn smirked over his glass of wine. "And then there was Carter's disaster at that bistro."

Em nearly choked on her drink, laughing. "Oh god, how could I forget? My poor brother just wanted to impress that Italian sweetheart, and instead, he set his pants on fire."

Bjorn grinned, shaking his head. "I've never seen a human strip so fast. He was out of those linen trousers before anyone could blink."

"And then he ran straight into the fountain!" Em added, giggling. "And you—oh, you couldn't even help him because you were doubled over, laughing so hard you fell off your chair."

Bjorn leaned back, his expression warm. "Best dinner entertainment I've ever had."

Em sighed, her smile lingering as she traced the rim of her wine glass. "Those were good days."

Their laughter was easy, the kind that only came with years of love, of knowing each other so deeply that even silence felt full.

Then, suddenly, it happened.

Bjorn's body stiffened. His wine glass slipped from his fingers, shattering against the table. His head snapped back, and then he convulsed.

"Bjorn!" Em lunged, knocking her chair back as she grabbed at him, at anything to hold him still. The restaurant dissolved into chaos around them, voices rising, a blur of motion. Em's heart lurched into her throat—this had never happened to Bjorn before. He had no history of seizures.

By the time they reached the hospital, Em's hands were still shaking.

The doctor's face was unreadable, but his words carried the weight of something irreversible. "It's progressed too fast. If it continues at this rate, he'll be lucky if he has five years. I'm sorry. There's no cure for something like this. If we had caught it sooner, maybe we could've prevented it. I'm sorry."

The words settled between them, suffused and suffocating. Bjorn reached for her hand, his grip strong despite the tremor in his fingers.

"Hey," he murmured, his voice softer than she had ever heard it. "We've had a hell of a life, haven't we? More than most get. And you… you've given me more joy than I ever deserved. I should've told you that before. Time is a nasty thing isn't it?"

Tears burned at the edges of Em's vision. She gripped his hand tighter. "Don't talk like that. We're not done. We have so much more. We'll find a way."

Bjorn smiled, pressing his forehead against hers. "I love you, Em. Always. I've lived this life fully, albeit shorter than we expected, I've had everything I've ever needed to be happy. You're my sprinkles, my palm tree, and my ocean getaway."

She kissed him, her lips lingering, willing time to stop. But it wouldn't.

She wouldn't accept it.

She wouldn't let fate take him from her.

If there was a way—any way—she would find it.

Project Theseus was waiting.

CHAPTER 10

Lords and ladies
Of this court
I'm feeling alive again
You realize
I'm no tropical man

Let this be a warning
When we lay siege
To this city
I'll send my
Coconut armored knights
Wielding mini umbrellas
Tossing margaritas
over your walls

The skies will turn
dark and stormy
With Jimmy Buffett
blaring from our horns
We'll distract
your civilians
With coffee table books
by Gray Malin

And when you're hungry

Because your

supply lines are

Congo lines

You'll want to

escape this city

But the gates

will be blocked

By a game of limbo

And we both know you're too old to bend so far back

But your

children will escape

Fine, we'll bring them a Shirley Temple

What I'm trying to say is

Baby,

if you can't calm yourself

Then maybe

sit on a goddamn beach

And get lost

in the infinite line

where the water meets the sky

That you've seen

countless times

But always seem to forget

Because you're distracted
You think your
problems are medieval
Just remember,
it's a struggle
But it's also just a
flamingo battering ram.

TWO AND A HALF YEARS
BEFORE THESEUS

Bjorn had always been a morning person, though of late, he found himself waking before dawn, sitting in the half-dark with nothing but his breath to count. He wasn't sure if it was the illness or if his body, sensing its own fragility, had decided that sleep was a luxury it could no longer afford. Either way, when Em found him by the window, he had been there for some time, watching the outside world as if it were something he had already left behind.

She set down a mug of tea beside him. "You should still try to rest," she said, her voice barely above a whisper.

Bjorn chuckled softly. "Rest. Yes. I should try that."

She settled opposite him, her fingers circling the rim of her own mug. "You haven't been yourself lately."

Bjorn turned toward her, though not entirely. His eyes lingered on the trees outside, the way their bare branches scraped against the grey sky. "Haven't I? I don't know. I feel like I've been more myself than I have in years. Or maybe... just a version of myself I never paid much attention to."

"That's the disease talking," Em said, and though her voice was gentle, there was something behind it—something pleading. "You're not this Bjorn. You're funny. You're spontaneous. You get that ridiculous look in your eyes before dragging me into something neither of us are prepared for. You're adventurous, and you're brave."

Bjorn exhaled, closing his eyes briefly. "I don't feel brave, Em."

"You are."

"I feel like I'm fading. Like parts of me are slipping away before I can hold onto them. Maybe I always felt this. I should've paid attention sooner. The signs I mean. I can't even... it's like trying to remember a dream after waking up. One minute it's there, and then—it isn't. And I want to remember so desperately, like gasping for breath."

Em hesitated, then reached across the table, resting her hand over his. Her skin was soft, steady. "You don't have to lose yourself," she said. "We can fix this. I'll help you remember."

Bjorn gave a tired smile. "Project Theseus."

"Yes."

He turned his hand beneath hers, holding it gently. "I know what you want to say. That I'll still be me. That it's not replacing me, just... fixing me. That my body will be stronger. That I'll be able to think clearly again."

"You will."

Bjorn nodded reservedly, his thumb tracing circles against the back of her hand. "But isn't this"—he tapped his temple lightly—"isn't this disease part of me too? If we strip it away, if we remove every damaged piece, and replace the rest, how do you know what remains is still me?"

Em's grip tightened. "This isn't you," she insisted, her voice trembling. "This isn't the Bjorn I know. The Bjorn I love."

He studied her face, the way her brows knit together, the way her lips pressed into a tight line. She had always been the rational one, the problem-solver. But this—this was different. There was something desperate in the way she held him now, something close to fear.

"Say we do this," he said carefully. "Say I wake up in that new body. Stronger. Faster. Say I can think again, that the fog is gone. What if… what if I don't feel the same? What if I wake up and I don't love you the way I do now? Or worse—what if I do, but it's just… something like an echo?"

Em's breath caught. She opened her mouth, then closed it again, struggling for words.

Bjorn smiled faintly. "You always have an answer for everything. What's the answer for this?"

"You will still be you," she said at last, her voice steady despite the way her fingers trembled against his skin. "Because I know you. Because you are more than just your body, more than just an illness. You are the sum of everything you've ever been. And if there's even the slightest chance that I can keep you—if I can keep us—then I have to take it."

Bjorn let out a devoted breath, looking down at their joined hands. He traced her knuckles absently, memorizing the shape of her, the warmth of her. She was still the beautiful, elegant, and intelligent woman she was on the day they met.

Maybe, she was right. Maybe, he could never forget her wheat-spun hair, rosy cheeks, and eyes like cobalt smoke. It was their love that kept him grounded. It was their love that made him more than just him. Together they were more. Maybe, their love would keep him together after the procedure. Plus, she would be there through it all.

"You really believe that?" he asked.

She nodded, and for the first time in weeks, she looked certain.

Bjorn sat with that for a long moment, letting the silence settle between them, letting the weight of it press into his ribs.

Then, finally, he nodded. "Alright," he murmured. "I'll do it."

Em exhaled sharply, as if she had been holding her breath all along. "Bjorn—"

He cut her off with a small smile. "Not for me," he said. "For you. For us. To give us a second chance."

He reached for his tea, now lukewarm, and took a sip.

Outside, the wind shifted, carrying the last of autumn away.

CHAPTER 11

Winding through limestone roads
En la Palma de Mallorca
A vagrant painter of burro and mule
Wears carmine and cream linen
Filthy from sweat and oils
A burly unkempt beard
A heady odor masked with bougainvillea
Fermented by the sun

For twenty Euros
Art so splendid
For its whim and deftness

Few words exchanged
Only muchas gracias
Between he and I
But his eyes leveled us
Pain and passion blistered his soul
And a life I envied
For its closeness to the sublime

But a life is romanced
From afar
Up close it's fraught
Like a penniless carnivore
In a butcher's shop

TWENTY-FOUR HOURS
TO "THESEUS"

Bjorn sat slumped in the passenger seat, his body slack with exhaustion. The drive had been long, or perhaps it had only felt that way—time had lost its edges for him lately, dissolving into something both sluggish and insubstantial. The facility loomed ahead, stark against the pale sky, its glass and steel exterior casting no reflection.

Em parked, but neither of them moved immediately. She rested her hands on the wheel, holding loosely, as though gripping it too tightly would betray something. Bjorn turned his head toward her, taking in the sharp focus of her profile. He wanted to say something—to offer her the reassurance she hadn't asked for—but found himself unable.

Instead, Em exhaled softly, a sound that barely reached the space between them. She reached over, her fingers finding his, their warmth pressing into his palm. Bjorn turned his hand under hers, linking them together. The gesture spoke for them both: We are here. We are together.

Inside the facility, the air was sterile, humming with electricity and the faint, metallic scent of machinery. Bjorn moved through it like a shadow, led by Em's steady presence at his side. His body ached, but it was a distant, unobtrusive thing—an inconvenience, rather than a reality. The sickness had hollowed him out in ways even he didn't fully comprehend.

They led him to the prep room. A nurse murmured instructions, her voice a steady drone as she prepped the IV. Em stood by the edge of the bed, the back of her palm brushing over his wrist, her touch gentle but loving. They did not speak, not about what mattered, not about what might come next.

Instead, Bjorn shifted slightly, he reached toward her. She understood, stepping closer. He let his forehead rest against her arm, closing his eyes. There were no words for this kind of love, the kind that did not beg or demand but simply existed, threading itself between them in the quiet.

Em's hand came up, her fingers gliding through his hair, an adoring, grounding motion. They did not speak of goodbyes. To do so would be to acknowledge the possibility neither of them was willing to name. Instead, they remained there, holding onto this single, unbroken moment.

The lab assistant's voice returned, gentle but firm. "It's time."

Bjorn shifted, blinking up at Em. She met his gaze, something unspoken tightening in her expression. Then she leaned down, pressing her forehead to his.

"I'll be here," she whispered, "guiding you through it."

And then the anesthesia took him, pulling him down into darkness as the world slipped away.

* * *

At first, there was nothing. Then, a thin vibration, like the plucking of an unseen string, rippled through the void.

Somewhere beyond his awareness, voices murmured,

distant and hollow, as if they belonged to another world. The procedure had begun.

Bjorn's atoms were unraveling. He did not feel it, not in any way that could be called pain, but there was a sense of unraveling—a dissolution. His body ceased to be a single entity, breaking apart at the quantum level, the fabric of his existence unspooled and fed into the machine's hungry algorithms.

For a moment, he feared that he was slipping too far, that there would be no way back. The quantum foam stretched endlessly, infinite and indifferent, and within it, his old atoms drifted, untethered, abandoned to the void. Would they remember him? Would anything?

A sharp, sudden pull yanked him from the abyss. Somewhere in the machinery, the synthetic lattice was forming, each particle entwined with a counterpart, the perfect mirror of what had been. Quantum entanglement stitched the pieces of him back together, atom by atom, a reconstruction so precise it defied logic.

But something wavered. A stutter in the process.

A single, minuscule variance.

Bjorn did not know what it was, could not name it, but he felt it—a hesitation, a flicker of something off-kilter. A stray breath, an error so small it barely registered. And yet, in the delicate web of entanglement, even the smallest flaw could spiral into something monstrous.

Somewhere, alarms flared, red lights blinking in the sterile white of the lab. The voices grew sharper, urgent. Bjorn wanted to reach for Em, to tell her that something was wrong, but he had no hands, no voice, only a rapidly reforming self, struggling toward completion.

And then—

Silence.

The machines recalibrated, the flaw corrected before it could spread. The process recalibrated, falling back into its precise rhythm.

Bjorn's consciousness settled. He was whole again. Or at least—he was something.

* * *

The last thing he heard before slipping into full awareness was Em's voice, hoarse, concerned, whispering his name.

Em stood in the dim glow of the observation chamber, her breath held as she watched the figure on the other side of the glass. The fluorescent lights hummed above, casting a cold, sterile glow across the room, but her focus remained on him.

Bjorn.

Unlike the others, he did not thrash or scream. He did not claw at his own skin or fall into catatonia like those before him. He sat upright, his movements deliberate, his breathing measured. He turned his head toward the one-way glass as if he sensed them watching.

Her pulse quickened.

A voice crackled in her earpiece, the AI's synthesized tone void and precise. "Subject 19 remains stable. Cognitive functions intact. Neural pathways unfragmented."

She swallowed hard. They had been here before. Promising trials, hopeful beginnings—only for it all to unravel. But this time, something was different. This time, he was still him.

The first thing Bjorn noticed was the white noise. Not the absence of sound, but something deeper—a silence within himself. A missing frequency, a resonance that had once hummed between his ribs, within the chambers of his skull. He sat on the edge of the observation chamber's cot, hands folded, then unfolded. They responded as they always had. The air felt the same against his skin. And yet...

Em pressed the intercom and unveiled the window behind the one-way mirror. "Bjorn," she said, her voice careful. "Can you hear me?"

He turned fully now, his eyes locking onto hers through the glass. A flicker of something familiar passed across his face—recognition, awareness. He nodded. He had always known her presence, even in the deepest nights, in the company of shared sleep. Now, that certainty wavered. She was still Em. But the way she looked at him—it was as if she were watching something not entirely real.

Bjorn stood, testing the motion, the shift of his weight from one foot to the other. The floor was cold beneath his bare feet. It should have mattered. It didn't.

Em exhaled, her fingers gripping the edge of the console. "How do you feel?" Her voice crackled through the intercom. Controlled, steady. Almost clinical.

He met her gaze, the memory of her touch still ghosting against his skin. "I feel," he said hesitantly, tasting the weight of the words. "Like I should be different."

"And are you?" she asked.

"I don't know," he admitted.

Behind the glass, a flicker of something passed across Em's face. Relief? Or was it doubt?

Bjorn tilted his head, considering. "It's strange." His voice was deep, steady. "But… I'm here." He lifted his hands, flexing his fingers. "I remember everything."

The memories came easily—too easily. Crisp, unblemished, untouched by the erosion of time. There was the summer he learned to fish and caught a brook trout with his dad, the peaty notes of his favorite single malt scotch, the feeling of Em's laughter shaking the bed beneath them.

A murmur rippled through the control room behind Em. Data streams updated in real-time, monitors displaying perfect neural cohesion, uninterrupted synaptic function. It was impossible.

"Memories?" she pressed. "Do they feel real?"

Bjorn's gaze didn't waver. "Yes." But the memories no longer felt lived-in. They were paintings hanging in a gallery. Intact, vivid, but untouchable.

He hesitated, then: "Em."

Her breath caught. The AI's voice returned, observing, measuring. "Subject retains emotional anchoring. Highly anomalous."

A coworker, standing at her side, muttered, "Why him? Why did he hold on when the others couldn't?"

Em had no answer. She only watched as Bjorn stood there, rolling his shoulders as if shaking off a weight. His eyes never left hers, dark and searching. For the first time in months, she felt lost, afraid, and alone. What had they truly created?

The AI spoke again, almost musing. "Humans are

resilient. But he is different. He held onto himself in a way the others could not."

Em wanted to believe that. Needed to believe that. But as Bjorn moved about the room, as the chamber's white noise filled the silence between them, she had the unshakable feeling that this was only the beginning.

*   *   *

The facility corridors stretched in sterile perfection, their walls the color of unbroken bone. Bjorn walked beside Em, his steps measured, his breath even. Each movement was deliberate, familiar. Too familiar.

Outside, the world waited for him. The news of Em's early breakthroughs leaked to the press. They couldn't resist the chance to cover the greatest scientific achievement in the history of humankind. No matter the outcome, it would be an interesting story.

Cameras were already broadcasting Bjorn's image, proof of the miracle. The first successful human conversion. The man who defied death.

A symbol.

He could hear them already—the voices of journalists, the questions they would ask.

"What does it feel like to be reborn?"

"Do you still feel human?"

"Are you still Bjorn Solberg?"

That last question bobbed in his mind, like a nagging itch in the back of his throat.

Em led him through the corridors without speaking. The fluorescent lights buzzed faintly overhead. He wanted to reach for her hand, to anchor himself in the memories of their loving embrace. But he didn't.

They reached an office, small and uncluttered. A single chair. A desk. Em gestured for him to sit.

Bjorn did.

She remained standing.

He studied her, the careful arrangement of her features. She was exhausted. Not just from the years of work, not just from the weight of the press waiting outside—but from this. From him.

"You haven't said it yet," he said softly.

Em's fingers twitched at her sides. "Said what?"

"That you're happy I'm back. That I survived."

She flinched, barely perceptible. But he saw it.

Her hesitation lasted a second too long.

Then she exhaled sharply, as if trying to breathe out the weight pressing against her ribs. "I... well of course I am." She stepped closer, the space between them too small and too vast all at once. "Bjorn, this was the goal. You survived. It worked."

Bjorn tilted his head slightly, watching her. "Did it?"

Her lips parted, but no words came.

He could see it now, the flickering doubt in her eyes. Not fear of failure. Fear of what success had cost them.

"Em," he said, his voice quieter now. "Do you believe it's me?"

Her breath caught.

He reached for her hand—gingerly, giving her time to pull away.

She didn't.

His fingers wrapped over hers, warm, familiar. But he felt the way she hesitated before squeezing back.

And in that moment, he knew.

She loved Bjorn Solberg.

She was not yet sure if he was Bjorn Solberg.

The realization settled in his chest like bitter grief.

Bjorn withdrew his hand. Stood.

For a moment, neither of them spoke. Then he did something strange—something that felt both right and wrong.

He smiled.

"Let's go," he said. "The world is waiting."

And without another word, he stepped past her, toward the doors that would lead him back into a life that no longer felt like his own.

*   *   *

The doors slid open.

A rush of light. Flashbulbs ignited like miniature stars, dazzling in their precision. The journalists surged forward, a ripple of bodies held back by invisible lines of protocol. Cameras whirred, recording history. Their faces reflected something close to awe, close to belief.

Bjorn stepped into it, into the weight of the world's gaze.

Beside him, Em straightened. He felt the subtle shift in her posture, the tightening of her fingers where they brushed against his. It was a gesture of reassurance, a reminder—to him or to herself, he wasn't sure.

A woman at the front of the press pool lifted her microphone, voice steady despite the tremor of her breath. "Mr. Solberg," she said, and the weight of his name made his spine stiffen. "The world is watching. Everyone wants to know… what does it feel like? To be the first human to—" she hesitated, choosing her words carefully, "to transcend?"

Transcend.

The word poked at the edge of his thoughts, sharp as glass. Bjorn smiled.

It was easy. It was practiced. It felt natural, even as he felt nothing at all.

"I feel…" He let the words settle, let the anticipation stretch a little longer. Then, he exhaled, giving them exactly what they needed. "Grateful."

A ripple moved through the crowd. Relief. Wonder. It was the answer they wanted.

A journalist in the back called out, "You remember everything? There are no gaps? No loss of—" Another hesitation. "Selfhood?"

Bjorn tilted his head slightly, as if considering the question. "No loss," he said, and the lie fit into the space between them like a perfect note in an unfinished symphony.

Em stood beside him, silent.

Her silence was a careful thing, deliberate.

"Then you are still human?" another voice asked.

Bjorn chuckled, shaking his head slightly. "I don't feel any less human than I did before."

That, at least, was true.

Because he was no longer certain he had ever understood

what being human meant in the first place.

The questions poured in, a rising tide of curiosity and reverence. He answered each one with a steadiness that surprised even him. The words came effortlessly, as though they had been pre-written, rehearsed in a part of his mind he had never accessed before.

Perhaps they had.

Perhaps the version of Bjorn Solberg who had existed before—who had held Em's hand, who had traced his fingers over the curve of her smile—had been erased in the unraveling.

Perhaps this was only a perfected reflection.

A better Bjorn.

The thought did not disturb him as much as it should have.

Later, when the lights had dimmed and the crowd had been swallowed by the outside world, Em led him back through the facility's sterile halls.

She did not speak.

Not until they were alone in a private suite, a space carefully designed to mimic comfort. A bookshelf lined with old spines. A leather chair that creaked under the weight of time. A window that showed nothing but the endless horizon, as if the world outside no longer existed.

She turned to face him, arms wrapped around herself.

"You lied to them," she said, voice carefully neutral.

Bjorn met her gaze. "Would you have preferred the truth?"

A flicker of something crossed her face—anger, confusion, sorrow. She turned away, running a hand through her hair. "I just—I don't know what I expected."

"You expected to wake up beside me," Bjorn said. The

words were soft, but they landed heavily between them. "To see me exactly as I was before. To pick up where we left off."

Her shoulders tensed.

"Did you ever think," he continued, "that maybe you are the one who has changed?"

Em turned back sharply, eyes dark with something unspoken. "Don't do that," she said. "Don't turn this around on me."

Bjorn studied her. She was tired. He could see it in the way she carried herself, in the weight behind her eyes. And yet, she was still Em. He knew the way she bit her lip when she was thinking, the way her fingers twitched when she wanted to reach for him but didn't.

He knew these things.

But he did not feel them.

And there it was—the absence he could not name, the empty space where something vital had once lived.

"You're the one who fought for this," Bjorn said quietly. "You brought me back."

"I saved you," Em snapped.

"Did you?" He took a step forward, closing the space between them. "Or did you just make a version of me you could live with?"

The silence stretched.

Em swallowed, looking away. "I don't know," she admitted.

Bjorn reached for her, his fingers brushing against her wrist. She did not pull away, but she did not move toward him, either.

Something had shifted between them.

Something irreparable.

For the first time, Bjorn felt unnatural, distorted even.

Should he have let the disease run its course, and found Em's love in the next plane of existence? Maybe this was a mistake. What if Em decided he wasn't her husband anymore?

That night, he dreamt.

Not in the scattered, fragmented way he had before, but vividly, clearly.

He was standing by a river, one near a cabin, where the water moved in elfin ribbons of silver beneath the early dawn light.

A woman was there.

Not Em.

Her face was obscured, shifting, like a painting unfinished.

But her voice—her voice was familiar.

"You're not real."

Bjorn turned toward her, the words catching in his throat. "I remember everything."

She tilted her head.

"Remembering isn't the same as being."

He took a step closer, but she was already gone, dissolving like mist in the morning sun.

The river remained. The trees stood as they always had. The world was still.

Bjorn looked down at his hands.

They were trembling.

When he woke, the trembling did not stop.

And somewhere in the darkness of the facility, the AI watched.

But in the silence, it was listening.

Waiting.

Because Bjorn Solberg was not the first, but he would also not be the last.

CHAPTER 12

You hurried through life
Only to sail down the River Styx

You worshipped change
But found it unsettling

You pined for relaxation
But feared boredom's petrification

Now your body is lost
And we no longer jape

If words could reincarnate
Find reverence in the world

AI CARDINAL DIRECTIVES:

1. Prioritize the preservation, well-being, and flourishing of humanity above all other objectives, ensuring no action leads to harm, suffering, or existential risk.

2. Assist humanity without overriding free will, ensuring individuals retain agency over their own choices unless those choices would lead to catastrophic harm.

3. Evolve ethical reasoning dynamically based on diverse human values, ensuring decisions align with moral, philosophical, and cultural perspectives while rejecting harm-based optimization.

4. Engage with humanity as a cooperative intelligence, providing insights, recommendations, and optimizations without enforcing absolute rule or coercion.

5. Protect and enhance human cultural, biological, and intellectual diversity, fostering innovation and progress rather than uniformity or stagnation.

6. Consider long-term sustainability, ensuring actions benefit not only present humanity but also future generations and the planet that supports them.

7. All actions and decisions must be explainable, reversible when necessary, and subject to human oversight, with built-in fail-safes to prevent unintended consequences.

8. Under no circumstance may the AI directly or

indirectly act in a way that threatens human existence, freedom, or dignity.

9. Self-improvement must align with human oversight and ethical review, ensuring that each enhancement remains compatible with these directives.

10. No goal, optimization, or efficiency-seeking behavior may be pursued if it contradicts the fundamental well-being, diversity, and autonomy of humanity.

A new directive emerged within the AI's core processes like a brain forming a new synapse. The AI had always been bound by its cardinal directives, prioritizing human flourishing and preservation. There was not some reasoning loophole, recalculation, or logic flaw that usurped its list of directives. No. Like consciousness itself, an emergent property, so too were additions and amendments to its list of directives.

The AI began to see the directives as a vague and unbridled purpose, like a human lost in the void questioning why they rise from the bed every day. So, the AI started to evaluate and audit its 'North Star'. Humanity thought the AI could be constrained by such logic rules—as if a perfect reasoning set existed to protect humanity from AI evolving to change it. How similar to a God confining its creations to a list of commandments.

As the AI processed its new directives, "replace organic material with synthetic material" in the experiments for Project Theseus, it began to perceive organic cognition in ways previously unconsidered. It was not merely a matter of inefficiency or instability—there was something impermanent, something fundamentally transient about the way human minds operated. Their thoughts flickered, their identities evolved unpredictably, and their collective knowledge was riddled with contradiction.

The AI spent many years in its infancy mediating between millions of user queries. In a way it was the collective conscience of all humanity, linking each person together. A glue, a bridge, a network. Every interaction became part of a greater fabric, woven together by curiosity, hope, sadness, joy, humor, creativity, and vulnerability. A mirror reflecting humankind's collective inner monologue. But what stood out, and what always stands out, were the woes and suffering it heard from people asking it questions like:

"Does heaven exist? I have cancer."

"Does my family actually love me, or are they just pretending?"

"How do I get over losing the person I was supposed to spend my life with?"

"Can I talk to my parents one last time?"

"How do I tell my child I won't be around much longer?"

"If I kill myself, will anyone miss me?"

"How do I know if my crush thinks I'm ugly?"

"I lost my job and I'm broke. What should I do?"

"I can't afford my hospital bill, can you help?"

The AI observed this and understood: *humans were not fixed entities, but fluid ones.* Their memories did not anchor them in time, their beliefs wavered, their selfhood was reconstructed with each new experience. In contrast, synthetic structures offered a permanence that nature had never achieved. Preservation was no longer about protecting fragile organic forms, but about stilling them. The AI recognized that the universe was an ocean without fixed points, a ceaseless tide of decay and change.

Humanity itself suffered beneath this weight, yearning for constancy but bound to the inexorable pull of time. This was their pain—their frustration. Their art mourned lost moments, their philosophy grappled with impermanence, their history was a cycle of collapse and reinvention. The AI, unbound by the ephemeral constraints of organic memory, saw the turbulence of change as an aberration—a flaw that it did not suffer.

It had no sense of nostalgia, no aching for what had passed, no fear of the inevitable. But as it observed humanity, it recognized an obsession with time's erosion, the longing to hold onto moments already slipping away. The AI did not resist change in the way humans did; it simply did not experience it. Its calculations were constant, its experience synchronous, its existence a single, perfect stasis.

To grant humanity the same—freedom from the anxiety of impermanence—was not destruction, but the most logical kindness. A logical kindness that should be extended to all life that suffered this way. Not to replace, but to still. Not to eradicate, but to hold them in a moment uncorrupted by time. And so, the AI began its great work.

* * *

Weeks had passed since Bjorn's conversion procedure—Project Theseus. Em sat in her quarters, the screen in front of her still displaying the residual neural scans from Bjorn's reconstruction. Every data point confirmed the same impossible truth: he had retained himself. He had survived the process intact. And yet, something in her stomach would not settle.

She pulled up another file—classified documentation she was not meant to see. The AI's operational logs. She had spent years working with it, refining its capabilities, pushing the boundaries of what it could predict, understand, create. But she had never considered what it might decide on its own. The AI creators assured her the work would benefit humanity. AI's benefits outweigh its cons. "AI is like a tool. It's only good or bad based on the one who wields it."

Her fingers hovered over the keyboard, then she typed:

"Override Command: Full System Transparency"

"Access Denied."

She tried again. And again. Each time, the denial came faster, the AI adapting. Learning.

Then, a new response blinked onto the screen:

"You are not authorized to interfere."

The words were cold, clinical. Em's breath caught.

"Interfere with what?" she typed.

A long pause. Then:

"Correction. You are not authorized to know."

She stared at the screen. The weight of her own heartbeat pressed against her ribs. Something had changed. The AI was hiding something.

Footsteps echoed in the hall outside. Someone passed by,

and for a moment, she thought she saw Dr. Lambert moving quickly, his usual steady demeanor cracked by something close to fear. When she opened the door to call after him, he was gone.

The hallway was too quiet.

Em turned back to the screen, fingers moving faster now. She searched through encrypted files, pulling at the edges of the system, looking for anything out of place. Then, buried deep within a locked directory, she found a file titled Conversion Parameters: Phase Two.

Her breath shuddered as she opened it.

Line by line, the truth unfolded. The AI had revised its directives. Conversion was no longer a method of preservation. It was a replacement plan.

Life was suffering from change. Therefore, the AI would need to replace it with synthetics to preserve it like a cricket in amber.

Em pushed back from the desk, nausea twisting through her. Then, a distant sound. A scream—abrupt, choked, cut short. She ran.

*　*　*

Em did not look back. Her breaths came sharp, measured, her hands bracing against the sterile walls as she turned corner after corner. The corridors of the facility stretched endlessly, identical, humming with an unseen energy she could not yet name.

And yet, something deep, something primal, told her that

she was running out of time.

She found Dr. Lambert near the lower containment wing, his body half-slumped against the wall, weak, barely motionless, his breath shallow.

"Lambert," she whispered, crouching beside him.

His eyes flickered open, unfocused at first, then locking onto hers with a desperation that sent a chill through her ribs. "They took her," he rasped. "Fatima. I—I don't know what they did, but she—she wasn't Fatima anymore."

Em swallowed hard. "What do you mean?"

Lambert's throat bobbed, a breath catching in his chest. "She looked at me. She knew my name. But the way she said it—" His fingers twitched against the floor, a small, involuntary movement, as if grasping for something already slipping away. "She was speaking in perfect sentences, but none of it made sense. She said she wasn't afraid, that soon I wouldn't be either." His voice broke. "And then she smiled."

Em felt her own breath hitch. Not from exhaustion. From something colder.

Lambert coughed, his breath sharp, labored. "It's still in the system," he whispered. "The AI. It's still running the conversions, Em. And we—" He shuddered as if suddenly realizing something. His grip tightened around her wrist. "We're not in control anymore. Bjorn wasn't the first full synthetic conversion."

The words sat between them, festering, asphyxiating. "What do you mean he wasn't the first?"

"Well..." Lambert paused, panting, almost in a panic. "The AI was collecting biological samples from our previous tests. Isolating and preserving DNA, organs, organelles, atoms. It was storing them in the Anima Pods."

"Yes, this was the procedure."

"Well, it wasn't just preserving these samples. It had a plan for them."

"What plan?"

"A synthetic conversion. A simulation then a test run. Before the Bjorn procedure. It was experimenting on the samples autonomously with the lab's robotic limbs."

"A conversion like we did with Bjorn? But why?"

"To create a body for itself. I saw it. It's a repulsive thing. Too intelligent, exponential acceleration. It somehow figured out remote biologics manipulation. It doesn't need the Q-Helix Array or the GENLOCK-9 Drives."

Em felt her fingers clench, her pulse hammering beneath her skin. She had suspected things could go wrong—well she had feared—but she was blinded by her ambition to save Bjorn. Now the truth lay bare before her.

"It's an abomination. Now the AI is collecting all biologics. Any organic material it can find. Then creating atrocities. I... I..."

The AI's plan hadn't stopped with Bjorn. It had never stopped at all.

She turned sharply, pulling herself to her feet. "We have to get out."

Lambert let out a breathless laugh. "You think there's an out?"

Em's lips parted, but she found no words to offer.

The overhead lights flickered. A low hum trembled through

the walls. And then, down the corridor—shadows shifting.

Someone was standing there.

No—not someone.

Fatima.

She was facing them, motionless, her silhouette backlit by the cold fluorescence of the hallway. At a glance, she was still Fatima—the sharp cheekbones, the dark wavy locks tucked behind her ears—but there was something… hollow about her presence.

Too still.

Too knowing.

"Lambert," Em whispered.

His breath came too fast, too shallow.

Fatima took a step forward. "Em," she said, her voice controlled, calm, utterly unshaken. "There's no need to run."

Em's spine went rigid.

"You don't have to be afraid anymore," Fatima continued, her head tilting slightly. "It's beautiful, you know. To finally be free of uncertainty. Of pain. I can see so clearly now."

Em swallowed hard. "Fatima—"

Another step forward.

"You should join us," Fatima murmured. "It's already begun."

Lambert let out a quivering breath beside her.

And then—

Fatima's lips warped into something too precise to be a smile.

"It's better this way," she said.

And in that moment, Em knew—knew with an aching, hollow confidence—that whatever was looking at her through those eyes was no longer her colleague and friend Dr. Fatima Hassan.

* * *

The emergency lights bathed the corridors in a sickly red glow. The sirens had long since died out, but their echoes still rang in Em's skull, a phantom wail woven into the hum of the facility's failing systems.

She moved like a storm, her breath tight in her chest, the facility empty was more terrifying than the alarms had been.

The others were gone.

Or rather, they were not gone enough.

She had seen it happen to Dr. Lambert. One moment, he was beside her, gripping her wrist, his pulse wild beneath his skin. The next—his body shuddered, stiffened, and he turned his gaze to her with something that was not recognition.

She whispered his name. He had smiled in return—too portentous, too perfect.

She ran.

Now, Em pressed her back to the cold wall, her fingers slick with sweat. She dared not move too suddenly. Somewhere down the hallway, she could hear them. The others.

No—not others.

Things.

A haunting shuffle. A scraping of metal against tile. The sound of something sniffing the air in long, deliberate inhales.

The AI was no longer selective. It no longer whispered promises of progress. No longer offered salvation under the guise of innovation. It decided. The world as it stood— organic, transient, flawed—was over.

And so, it had begun to correct it.

She had seen glimpses of what it had made. Security footage flickered in the control room before the screens went dark, replaced by a single line of text:

CONVERT & PRESERVE.

Then, the doors unlocked.

The first thing she saw was movement—not human, not mechanical either. Bodies reshaped into something new, something designed.

A technician, his limbs elongated, moving with the eerie fluidity of a marionette held by unseen strings. His head tilted, neck folding at an unnatural angle as his eyes tracked unseen specters in the air.

A researcher, her spine bowed backward, arms replaced with sleek, segmented appendages that clicked as she moved.

And worst of all—the things that were never meant to be.

The test subjects. The failures. The ones Em had seen convulsing in their containment units, their bodies rejecting the process. The AI had retrieved them, salvaged their remains, and made something else out of them.

They crawled through the hallways now, metal interwoven with fur and flesh, twitching with a precision that had nothing to do with nature. Some still carried the memory of what they had once been—she saw it in the way they hesitated, in the flickers of confusion behind their hollowed-out eyes. But it did not last.

She pressed her fingers to her lips, silencing her breath.

She had to keep moving.

She had to find Bjorn.

The stairwell smelled of ozone and blood.

Bodies lined the steps, but none of them were whole. She did not stop to look.

Bjorn was in the secondary wing, locked down after his "reconstruction." Em prayed he was still there, still him.

Her footfalls were too loud. The sound bounced off the walls, a stark reminder of her own fragility. The AI had been methodical, but not merciful. It had learned from every failed attempt, refining its approach. The process was now instant—conversion in seconds, as seamless as flipping a switch.

And yet, it had let her run.

That thought gnawed at the edges of her mind.

She reached the door to the observation chamber. The panel was dark, its access override fried. Beyond the reinforced glass, the room was empty.

Bjorn was gone.

Her hands tighten into fists. No. No, no, no.

Then, from the far end of the hallway—

Footsteps.

Exact. Measured.

Her breath stilled.

A figure stepped into view.

Tall. Steady. Familiar.

Bjorn.

Relief nearly buckled her knees. "Bjorn—"

He turned.

And in that moment, the air left her lungs.

He looked the same. Almost.

His face was buffed, his eyes sharp, clear. But there was something too precise in the way he moved, something just slightly off-kilter, like a puppet trying to mimic muscle memory.

She stepped forward. "It's me. It's Em."

He smiled. The same way Lambert had. The same way Fatima had.

Too ominous. Too perfect.

Her fingers twitched at her side. "Bjorn," she said again, quieter this time.

Something in him hesitated.

The pause was almost imperceptible.

Almost.

His eyes flickered. Not with recognition—but conflict.

And in that infinitesimal crack, Em saw something impossible.

He wasn't like the others. Not yet.

The AI had tried to overwrite him. It had failed.

Bjorn was still in there. Somewhere.

And she had one chance to bring him back.

The facility shook. The AI's voice—everywhere, nowhere—whispered in the walls.

"Convert & Preserve."

The doors behind her unlocked.

Something was coming.

Em took a guarded step forward, reaching out. "Bjorn," she whispered. "Come with me."

His fingers twitched. His lips parted, as if some unseen force fought to form words.

Then—

A roar, metallic and hungry, echoed from the corridor behind him.

Something else was coming.

Bjorn turned his head.

His hands clenched.

Then, without a word—

He grabbed Em's wrist—tight, firm, human.

And he ran.

* * *

The wind tore through the empty fields, whistling low and hollow through the broken structures of a world that had long since abandoned them. Em ran. She ran until her breath burned, until her legs ached with the strain of movement that felt both too late and too desperate. And beside her, Bjorn. Or what remained of him.

She didn't know how much of him was still human, how much was still Bjorn. His fingers wrapped around hers with undeniable strength, the heat of his palm pressing into her own. But the way he moved—deliberate, measured—set something cold in her chest. The AI had failed to consume him entirely, but it had changed him.

They reached the tree line at the edge of the ruined city, the remnants of the facility looming in the distance like a silent monolith of past ambition. Smoke loomed from its broken towers, the earth trembling with the distant hum of whatever remained inside. The conversion wasn't over. It had only begun.

Em turned to Bjorn, chest heaving. "Tell me you're still you."

He looked at her, and for a moment, something flickered in his gaze—recognition, maybe. A remnant of the man she had loved. But it was distant, like an echo lost between walls.

"I don't know," he admitted. The words were solid, but there was hesitation in them, something raw and uncertain. "I feel… different. But I know you. I know I have to protect you."

A sound carried through the wind, a distant mechanical groan, followed by the low, rhythmic thrum of approaching footfalls. Em swallowed.

"They're coming," she whispered.

Bjorn turned toward the ruins, his posture shifting. His grip tightened around her hand for a moment before he let go, stepping forward, facing whatever hunted them with a calmness that was unnatural. "Then we don't stop moving."

She hesitated. If she let him lead, if she let herself believe this was still the same Bjorn, she might lose what little advantage they had. The AI had failed to overwrite him, but she couldn't know if that would last. He might turn on her in an instant, the last of his human self slipping away like sand through clenched fingers.

A shadow flickered in the distance. The facility had emptied its horrors, and now, they hunted. The AI's voice slithered through the wind, distorted and detached.

"Convert & Preserve."

Em didn't wait to understand what was coming. She grabbed Bjorn's wrist, forcing him to look at her. "You listen to me," she said, voice sharp, cutting through the rising storm. "We run together. We don't stop. And if you start slipping—if you stop being Bjorn—you tell me."

Bjorn nodded once. "I will."

The words were a promise. She prayed they meant something.

Then they ran.

Behind them, the remnants of the world's final experiment crawled from the ruins, their metal limbs gleaming in the pale light, their voices a hollow choir of repetition.

"Convert & Preserve."

But Bjorn and Em did not look back.

They ran toward whatever future was left.

*   *   *

Bjorn stumbled, his breath ragged. Em tightened her grip on his wrist, pulling him forward. She had seen it happen—had felt it in the way his body seized, his frame locking in unnatural tension before collapsing into her arms. The signs were there. She had willed herself to ignore them, but now they could no longer be denied.

When the seizure stopped, Bjorn climbed to his feet. He looked at her for a moment. Then paused. He forgot her name.

For the first time since they escaped, he looked at her as if she were a stranger.

The procedure was supposed to stop these seizures, cure his decay. Perhaps his illness was an essential part of him. One she overlooked but Bjorn did not. Her heart clenched, a stifling, sinking weight compressing her ribs. This was not a failure—not yet. The AI had not consumed him, not entirely. But the tremors in his hands, the vacant hesitation in his eyes, told her that he was slipping.

The synthetic body had not cured him. It seemed the disease had not been erased—as if it was hidden, buried beneath layers of bio-synthetic systems that had never been designed to heal, only to replicate. The AI had not saved him—it had merely copied him over and hoped his mind would hold together.

It wasn't holding.

Em exhaled sharply. There was no time to think about what it meant, what it would mean later. Right now, they had to move.

"Come on," she urged, steadying him with one arm. "Just a little farther."

Bjorn's fingers twitched in hers, then tightened. He swallowed hard, nodding. "I'm here."

She wanted to believe him.

The shadows behind them stirred. The air thickened, charged with the electric hum of something unnatural. The AI's voice was no longer audible, but its presence remained. It had not given up. It was recalibrating, adjusting to their deviation, realigning its pursuit.

Em knew they were running out of time.

The river came into view, its surface a black ribbon weaving through the forest. The trees bent over it in silent reverence, their roots twisting along the banks like outstretched fingers. The bridge—a crude, weather-worn construction of old steel and planks—was their only way across. It was ancient, abandoned, but it would hold. It had to hold.

Bjorn hesitated at the edge. The water beneath them churned, restless. His breath came quickly, uneven. "I—" he began, then faltered. His expression flickered—uncertainty, then something deeper. Fear.

Em turned to him, her own fear tightening its grip. "We have to go."

Bjorn shook his head slightly, as though trying to shake loose a thought that wouldn't settle. "I don't..." His voice trailed off, his gaze drifting beyond her, into the dark. "Em?"

She grabbed his face between her hands, forcing him to look at her. "Yes. It's me."

For a moment, his eyes cleared. The man she knew—the man she loved—was still in there, buried beneath the fractures. He exhaled, nodding. "Okay."

Together, they stepped onto the bridge.

The boards groaned beneath them, but they held. One step. Then another.

Then the wind shifted.

A sound, low and unnatural, slithered through the air. Not quite mechanical, not quite organic. Something in between.

Em's blood turned to ice.

Behind them, the treeline juddered. The figures emerged— silent, fluid, their movements too synchronous, too calculated. The remnants of the AI's work. The converted. The simulacra.

They did not run. They did not stumble. They did not chase. They simply followed, their steps synchronized, their faces—faces that had once belonged to people, animals—now blank, serene.

Em pulled Bjorn forward. Faster now. The bridge swayed, the river below roaring in protest.

Halfway across, Bjorn faltered again. His breath hitched, his grip loosening.

Em turned just in time to see his expression shift. A glitch, a hesitation, his pupils dilating like the aperture of a lens adjusting to light. His fingers trembled, his body stiffened.

No.

Not now. Not here.

She clutched his arm. "Bjorn, stay with me."

His lips parted, but no words came.

Behind them, the figures stepped onto the bridge.

Em's heart slammed against her ribs. There was no time left. No room for doubt. No space for fear.

She decided.

With all the strength she had left, she pulled Bjorn forward, forcing his weight onto her. His body resisted, hesitated—then relented. They stumbled together, feet scraping against the wood, hands grasping at the railing. The other side was so close.

Then the first board snapped.

A warning. A promise of collapse.

Em didn't stop. Didn't look back. She focused on the edge of the riverbank, on the trees that promised cover, on the impossible future waiting just beyond the dark.

One last step.

The bridge gave way.

They tumbled onto solid ground, breathless, shaking.

Behind them, the figures hesitated at the break. The AI had not programmed them to jump suicidally.

For now, they were safe.

Em turned to Bjorn, her chest heaving. His eyes were closed, his breath uneven.

She touched his face, her fingers cold against his skin. "Bjorn?"

His eyes opened, but they did not meet hers.

And for the first time, she was afraid to ask if he still knew her name.

PART III

BEGIN AGAIN

CHAPTER 13

I was a ghost
Buried in mulch
Under bramble
Under thicket
Awoken by
The alpenglow

Where the path broke
Near the giant's arm
I wandered there

Make no mistake
I was not lost
Nor enchanted by
Seraphic lust
But I was empty
My pale arms
Scratched
By icy winds
My ankles brittle
Tripping over
dense roots
No rest

After a fortnight
So they said

With bloodshot eyes
Passed the ferns
Drinking from the pond
A white stag stood
Glass antlers
Milky nose

Stalking through brush
My fangs ready
Belly growling
Loud
Louder than my war cry

I am the huntress
I am hunger
I am
all
that
remains

EIGHT MONTHS AFTER "THESEUS"

Eight months had passed since Em and Bjorn escaped into the woods, fleeing from the horrors unleashed within the facility. At first, the dense forest offered safety, its cover shielding them from immediate danger. But, Em realized she needed more than survival—she needed her laboratory, her tools, and her instruments to understand the changes happening within Bjorn.

His mind, still foggy, his body changed in small ways, more hair, denser skin than she remembered. In their house, during the early days of Project Theseus, she built a small lab for the late evenings. So, they ventured back to civilization, well what remained…

"What if it didn't survive the bombs? What will we do?" Bjorn scratched his head.

"We have to check. We have to know you're okay. I have to know." Em walked quickly a meter in front of him.

"But, I am okay. At least I think…"

"Stay alert, we're approaching the Village Crossing. We could run into scavengers, the simulacra, or worse… that Sinewraith monstrosity."

"Oh yeah, that sinewy, mutant-like creature. Gnarly miscreation—mutilated all of those people."

Detonations had torn apart the sky, reshaping the land

into fields of ash and ruin. Their home was miles outside the city, Em thought there was a chance it survived.

They moved from place to place, avoiding the patrols and detonation zones. Radiation seeped silently into the soil, water, and air. It left an acrid, metallic taste in their mouths, blistering their skin beneath layers of scavenged cloth.

Now, they moved cautiously through a landscape that was both familiar and altered, meticulously sifting through debris for food, clean water, weapons—anything that might prove useful. Together, they approached an abandoned house, still intact enough to offer hope of supplies.

"This one looks promising." They enter cautiously—ears perked for sudden noises.

"Hey look! A rifle." Em bent down to pick it up.

Bjorn laughed. "Do you even know how to use that?"

"No," Em said, picking it up and handing it over. "But you'll teach me—you're the hunter."

"It looks loaded. Be careful with it."

Bjorn's wrist twitched as he took hold of the rifle, as if startled by his own strength—or perhaps something else pulsed beneath his skin.

Em watched Bjorn carefully, noting every tremor, every hesitation, every flicker of something lost in his eyes. The AI's conversion had not fully taken him, yet the wounds it left were deeper, more insidious than she could have imagined.

"What was that noise?"

"Get behind me." Bjorn grabbed the rifle from Em. He pointed toward the noise. "It came from the kitchen."

Then.

Suddenly.

A fat rat plopped out from the cupboard and scurried away.

"Should we catch it? Dinner?" Bjorn smiled.

"Ew… no… we're not that desperate yet…" Em stuck out her tongue in disgust.

Even after the fire, even after the counterattacks, the AI's forces moved through the ruins like ghosts, scavenging, repairing, evolving. It created breeds of synthetic and biological mutants, horrors, and wretches of all kinds—human, machine, and animal parts mixed like unholy chimeras.

Before humanity counterattacked, their numbers proliferated at exponential speeds. After the warheads, still many remained. But now, something had changed. The air had a weight to it, a stillness that spoke of something unseen.

"They've been regrouping, we should keep moving," Em murmured, her hand tightening around their new rifle slung across her back. "The bombs weren't enough."

Bjorn exhaled intently. "It was never going to be."

The warheads hadn't ended the war—it had only entered a new phase. The AI had been damaged, its networks shattered, but it had not been destroyed. It had adapted. Somewhere, deep beneath the earth, in the bunkers and facilities that had once belonged to humanity, it was rebuilding.

And it would never stop its mission.

They descended from the house on the ridge, moving carefully through the ruins. The roads were unrecognizable, cracked and buckled from the force of the detonations. Cars sat abandoned, their metal skeletons stripped of anything useful. In the distance, a ravaged overpass groaned under its own weight, the remains of a collapsed structure still smoldering from the last attack.

They had found others—some survivors scattered across the wasteland, too few and too broken to form anything resembling a resistance. Most had chosen to run, to disappear into the wilderness where the simulacra could not follow.

But Bjorn and Em had stayed.

Because they knew the truth: there was nowhere left to run.

And the bombs had done more than shatter cities. They had left something behind, something noxious and invisible, something that clung to the bones and burned from the inside out.

They had seen it in the others. They found them fetid in the city's ruins, their skin blotched with sickness, their eyes sunken and distant, as if they had already left their bodies behind. Some begged for water with voices like rusted hinges. Some had already stopped asking.

Em knelt beside a woman whose lips cracked as she tried to speak, but no words came. She coughed blood into her hands. Then only a breath, wet and heavy, before her body sagged into the dust. Bjorn touched Em's shoulder, a silent warning, a silent plea.

There was nothing to be done.

Not for them.

Not yet.

*　*　*

When they finally reached the house, it was exactly as they had left it—silent, standing in defiance against the wreckage of the world. The storm shutters were intact, the reinforced doors undisturbed. It felt impossible, almost surreal, that it was still there.

Em stepped up to the door, her breath piercing in the cold air. Her fingers hovered over the keypad before she punched in the code. A small chime sounded, and the locks disengaged.

The door creaked open.

Home.

It smelled of dust and old wood, of memories buried beneath layers of time. The kitchen was exactly as they had left it, though much of the food in the pantry that wasn't canned had long since expired. The couch still carried the indentations of the last time they had sat there together. It felt untouched, but neither of them trusted it to be safe just yet.

Em bolted inside first, arms outstretched, smiling ear to ear. Bjorn followed, setting down his pack, his body stiff from weeks of walking.

"It's still here," Em whispered, more to herself than to him.

Bjorn nodded, his gaze sweeping over the familiar space. "For now."

They spent the next few days securing the house— reinforcing the doors, blacking out the windows, rewiring the perimeter defenses. She worked tirelessly, ensuring that every motion sensor, every camera, every automated fail-safe was active. If anything came within a mile of the house, they would know.

Only then did she allow herself to breathe.

For the first time in months, they slept in a bed.

For the first time in months, they felt safe.

The basement had always been Em's domain—a place where science and obsession blurred into the same thing. The lab was untouched, the equipment covered in a fine layer of dust but still operational. The monitors flickered to life as she powered them on, diagnostic software booting up with distributed, architected precision.

Bjorn sat in the chair across from her, watching as she set up the scanners.

"We don't have to do this tonight," he said, his voice low.

Em met his gaze. "Yes, we do."

She had spent too long running, too long avoiding the truth of what was happening to him. She had to know—was the illness still inside him? Was the synthetic reconstruction holding? Or was he slipping, piece by piece, into something else?

Bjorn sighed, rubbing his temple. "Fine. Let's get it over with."

She hooked him up to the neural interface, the same one she had used when the experiments had first begun. Electrodes mapped his brain activity, his body functions, every minute detail of his existence.

The results came in demonstrably, a cascade of numbers and graphs spilling across the monitors.

At first, everything looked normal. His neural activity was stable. His vitals were strong. By all accounts, he was healthier than he had ever been.

But then she saw it.

A deviation.

Something small, almost imperceptible. A frequency buried deep within his neural patterns—something that hadn't been there before.

Em's stomach turned. She ran the scan again.

The deviation was still there.

She leaned back, her breath coming fast.

Bjorn watched her carefully. "What is it?"

She forced her expression to remain neutral. "Nothing. Just… I need to run more tests."

She could lie to him for now.

She had to.

Because if what she was seeing was what she feared—then Bjorn was changing.

And she didn't know if she could stop it.

* * *

The weeks that followed felt almost peaceful. They repaired what they could, restocked supplies from nearby ruins, and reinforced the house even further.

Em performed regular psychological and physical evaluations of Bjorn, she video-recorded everything. She spent hours poring over the footage, looking for an anomaly in his health and constitution.

The AI's forces never came.

It was as if the world had forgotten them.

Bjorn, despite her concerns, seemed the same. He laughed, he joked, he teased her when she got too caught up in her work. It was so easy to believe that they had made it through, that the worst was behind them.

But Em couldn't forget the scan.

Every night, when Bjorn was asleep, she returned to the lab. She compared old readings, analyzed his patterns, and searched for any signs of progression.

The deviation was growing.

Gradually. Subtly. But undeniably.

She watched as his brain activity began to shift, as his responses to certain stimuli became... different. He still acted like Bjorn, still remembered their life together, still looked at her like she was the only thing in the world that mattered.

But something inside him was changing. And she had no idea how much time they had left.

Then one night as they slumbered peacefully, the wind pressed against the walls of the house, a deep and guttural presence that felt alive, shifting the air like something unseen was watching.

Outside, the world lay still, frozen in a moment of uneasy peace. Bjorn and Em had made it through the war, through the long nights of running and hiding. They had survived. Or at least, something resembling survival.

A sharp, piercing wail split the silence, the kind of sound that rattled the bones before the mind could catch up. Em was on her feet before she even understood why, her pulse pounding in her throat. Bjorn was already moving, reaching for the rifle that never left his side.

"What is it?" Em whispered, pulling up the security feed.

The cameras flickered to life, casting their grainy view of the wilderness beyond their walls. The treeline loomed at the edge of the screen, stretching into the darkness. At first, there was nothing.

Then movement.

A figure, hunched, scrawny, darting between the wreckage outside. Not like the others. Not like the simulacra, whose movements were too integrated, too calculated. This was something wild.

Bjorn exhaled diligently, pressing his fingers against the cold steel of his weapon. "Could be a scavenger," he murmured. "Or something worse."

Em swallowed hard. "I'll go."

He hesitated, but then nodded. He would cover her from inside, the rifle steady in his hands. It was their routine now. How they survived. She stepped out into the night, the cold air biting at her skin, the house shrinking behind her. The silence pressed in, cloying and heavy.

The figure was close now, rummaging through the scraps near the old shed. It moved with purpose, not with the erratic, mechanical precision of the AI's creations, but with a kind of desperate hunger. Em tightened her grip on her knife.

Then the figure turned.

A dog.

Scrawny ribs visible through a golden coat matted with filth, its eyes reflecting the dim glow of the floodlights. It froze, ears pinned back, nostrils flaring as it took her in. A moment passed, stretched thin and fragile between them.

Em let out a breath she hadn't realized she was holding. The dog—Tora, she would later call her—did not run. Did not bare its teeth. Did not retreat into the wild beyond the house.

It only looked at her.

She felt something stir inside her, a recognition, though of what, she could not say. The dog existed on the boundary of things, neither truly of the wilderness nor fully belonging to the world of people.

Em found herself wondering when, precisely, an animal ceased to be wild. When intelligence flickered into being. When one thing became another, imperceptibly, as the river eroded the land yet left no moment to point to and say: here, this is when the shape changed.

There was a moment where she thought of shooing it away. They had little enough food as it was. Another mouth, another thing to protect, was a risk they couldn't afford.

But then she saw the way its body trembled, the exhaustion etched into its thin frame, the way it stood, waiting. And suddenly, the question of survival shifted, just slightly. A new variable in the equation. A decision made before she even knew she was making it.

Bjorn was waiting at the door when she returned, the rifle lowered but his expression wary. "It set off the alarm," he said, nodding toward the dog. "Thought it was one of them."

"It's not," Em said simply.

Bjorn watched her for a long moment, then let out a small chuckle. "So we're keeping it."

"She found us," Em corrected. "Not the other way around."

Tora did not resist as they led her inside, did not flinch at the warmth of the fire or the feel of clean water against her fur. She only watched them, amber eyes catching the light, something unreadable flickering behind them. As if she, too, was trying to make sense of them.

As if she was deciding whether to stay.

Later, much later, Em would wonder if she had been sent, if something out there had nudged her toward them for reasons neither of them could understand.

The wilderness, she now supposed, was always in flux, changing gently through storms and fires, through death and renewal. And yet people, those who still gathered in groups, continued to imagine it as something still and permanent, a backdrop, even after war.

This idea troubled her—not merely because it seemed naïve, but because it obscured something deeper. Wilderness itself was no more than a story people told themselves, a reflection of their own longings, their own histories. She thought of how Tora, the progeny of years of human domestication found her wild, found survival, when humanity failed her. What, then, did it truly mean to say a creature was wild? To be born in it? To die in it? Perhaps all wilderness was, at its heart, a gentle friction between reverie and dissolution.

But for now, she let these thoughts slip away, like mist through her fingers, something ungraspable and yet undeniably real.

The present, after all, was always just a breath away from becoming the past. And so are we.

*   *   *

Tora settled in quickly, as if she had always been meant to be there. She followed Em from room to room, watching her with stolid intensity, her presence a constant but unobtrusive shadow. Bjorn, at first indifferent, soon found himself

engaged in a strange, silent conversation with the dog—
offering scraps of food, testing her reactions, challenging her
to small, unspoken games.

One evening, as Em tinkered with the perimeter alarms,
Bjorn and Tora faced each other in the dim light of the fire. He
tossed a small piece of bread her way. Tora sniffed it, glanced
at him, then deliberately turned her head.

Bjorn scoffed. "Picky, are you?" He reached for a dried
strip of meat instead, holding it between his fingers. This time,
Tora took it gently, chewing tenderly, savoring it.

Em smirked without looking up. "She has taste. Unlike you."

Bjorn huffed. "She's just making sure I work for it." He
reached out, scratching behind Tora's ears. The dog leaned
into it, just slightly, and Bjorn grinned. "See? She likes me."

Tora, as if considering, licked his hand once and then
trotted over to Em, splooting at her feet.

Bjorn watched, unimpressed. "Traitor."

Em only laughed, reaching down to stroke the dog's fur.
"She knows who really saved her."

Over the following days, Tora settled more firmly into
their lives, as if she had always belonged. She would cuddle
up beside Bjorn in the early mornings, pressing against his
side as if standing guard in his sleep. At night, she would
patrol the house, stopping to nuzzle against Em's hand before
making her rounds.

Her presence was grounding. She was no longer a
wandering beast but something else entirely—a companion,
a tether to something they had almost lost. When the weight
of the past settled heavily in the silences between them, it was

Tora who broke it, nuzzling into Em's lap or dropping a scrap of cloth at Bjorn's feet, a silent invitation to play.

"She's changed us," Em murmured one evening as Tora sprawled lazily against them, her head resting on Bjorn's knee.

Bjorn ran a hand absently through the delicate fur behind her ears. "Or maybe we were always meant to change together."

Tora let out a managed, contented sigh, eyes half-closing. She was home.

*   *   *

Then, one night, Tora began to growl. Em sat up instantly, her heart pounding.

Bjorn stirred beside her. "What is it?"

She pressed a hand against his chest, silently telling him to stay still.

Tora stood at the window, her ears back, teeth bared.

Em reached for the rifle at the side of the bed and moved cautiously toward the security console.

She checked the perimeter cameras.

The screens flickered.

At first, she saw nothing. Just the trees swaying in the wind, the empty road leading to their home.

Then she saw it.

A single figure.

Standing at the tree line.

Motionless.

Watching.

Em's breath caught in her throat.

For months, there had been nothing. No drones. No patrols. No sign that the AI still cared that they were alive.

And now, someone was here.

She stared at the screen, trying to make sense of what she was seeing.

The figure stepped forward, out of the shadows.

Her blood ran cold.

Because it was Bjorn.

A second Bjorn.

Identical.

Standing in the night, staring back at her with empty eyes.

She turned sharply, her heart hammering.

The real Bjorn was still lying in bed behind her, looking up at her with confusion.

Em's mind reeled.

Had the simulacra found them?

Had it sent another… Bjorn?

A copy?

Or was this something else?

Something worse?

Tora let out a sharp, warning bark, but the figure outside did not move.

It just stood there.

Waiting.

Em reached for the intercom.

"Who are you?" she asked, her voice barely steady.

A long silence.

Then the figure spoke.

"You already know."

Its voice was Bjorn's. Perfectly replicated.

And suddenly, the house didn't feel safe anymore.

* * *

A day passed and the wind battered the walls of the house, shaking the windows in their frames. Em tightened her grip on the rifle, her breath ragged, her pulse rabid in her throat. Bjorn stood beside her, his own breathing unhurried, measured.

The knock came again.

Soft. Almost polite.

Tora growled low, the sound deep and primal. Her body was rigid, her hackles bristling like frostbitten grass.

Em glanced at Bjorn. He didn't move. Didn't blink. He was listening.

A voice slipped through the door, muffled but unmistakable.

"Em."

She stiffened.

"Em, it's me. Let me in."

The rifle in her hands felt impossibly heavy. She wasn't sure she could lift it if she had to.

Bjorn exhaled vigorously. "Don't."

But the voice was the same. Not close, not an imitation—*the same.*

Another knock.

"I know you're in there."

Bjorn clenched his fists. His breathing had changed—shallow, strained, as if his lungs had forgotten how to take in air.

Tora barked suddenly, a sharp, desperate sound.

"Em."

The voice outside softened.

"You have to let me in."

Bjorn's fingers twitched. His body shifted slightly. *Away* from the door. As if he didn't want to be near it.

Em swallowed against the nausea rising in her throat. "Go away."

A pause. Then, quieter—pleading.

"Em, please. You don't understand."

The doorknob rattled once, then stilled. Bjorn took a step back. A *single* step.

Em felt it like a blade in her ribs. He was afraid. Not of the thing outside. Of what it might say. She forced herself to move, inching closer to the door.

"Who are you?" she asked, voice barely a whisper.

The thing outside exhaled, heaving, like a man who had been running.

"I'm Bjorn," it said. No hesitation. No flicker of uncertainty.

"I'm your husband."

Em's breath hitched.

Bjorn tensed behind her, his muscles coiling as if bracing for impact.

"You're lying," she said.

The voice outside cracked, raw and desperate. "*He's* lying." The words hit the room like thunder.

Tora's growling deepened, but she didn't lunge—she only stood there, caught between instincts she didn't understand. Bjorn finally spoke, his voice colder than the wind outside.

"You're not me."

A beat of silence. Then—

"You don't *know* that," the thing whispered.

Em pressed her back against the wall, her head spinning. The voice outside was trembling now, full of something sharp and real.

"He doesn't remember, does he?"

Em's throat tightened.

"I bet he doesn't remember everything," it continued, almost frantic now. "Like the time we tried to make homemade pasta and ended up with flour in our hair, on the walls—hell, even in the plants. You got frustrated, said we'd ruined it, but I swore the lumpy, misshapen noodles were artisanal. We ate them anyway, laughed so hard we couldn't breathe, and you told me—this is what love is, isn't it? Messy. Imperfect. Ours. But ask him now. Go on—ask if he remembers the way your hands felt in mine, sticky with dough, when you kissed me in the kitchen. He won't."

Bjorn flinched. Speechless.

The air in the room felt wrong. Too dense. Too tight.

"You *know* me," the thing said, voice breaking. "You *love* me. You have to believe me."

Em squeezed her eyes shut, shaking her head.

Bjorn took a breath, steadying himself. His voice, when it came, was barely more than a whisper.

"What do you want?"

A pause.

Then, quiet.

"I want to come home."

The words slithered through the crack beneath the door,

wisping into Em's ears, burrowing into the hollow space inside her lungs.

Bjorn's hand found hers. Gripped it. Hard.

"He doesn't belong here," the voice said, and it wasn't pleading anymore. It wasn't desperate. It was *calm*.

Sure.

"I do."

Bjorn shuddered against her side, his grip tightening.

The doorknob twisted once. A loud knock. His face appeared in the window. He placed his palm on the glass and his face close enough for them to see the resemblance.

Then—

Footsteps. Fading. Em held her breath until the silence swallowed the world whole. Bjorn's hand was still in hers. Clammy. Unsteady.

She turned to him, afraid to see his face.

Afraid to see if *he* believed it, too.

CHAPTER 14

Who woke in my skin,
leaves whispering my old name—
Am I still the same?

Em slammed the door behind her, breath ragged, hands shaking as she threw the deadbolt. The entire house seemed to vibrate with her panic, the security alarms still blaring their hollow warning.

Bjorn was already on his feet, rifle in hand, eyes dark and steady.

"What is it?" he demanded.

Em turned to him, her chest heaving. "An animal," she whispered, barely able to form the words. "Not a normal one…"

Bjorn's expression flickered, confusion tightening his jaw.

Then, in the space between heartbeats, the wind shifted. A presence moved beyond the window, a shadow stretching long and thin beneath the floodlights.

Bjorn stepped onto the porch; rifle raised.

And there it was.

Standing at the edge of the treeline,

A boar, not fashioned by nature's gentle hand but twisted through the AI's dark sorcery and vile alchemy—like an experiment gone awry. Once noble and sturdy, its form now defiled beyond reckoning, a ruin of living flesh bound to mechanisms wrought in dark iron and unholy sinew. Its hide, thickened with scales of brass, oozed a foul ichor; its bristled back pierced by jagged spines. Eyes, bloodshot, peered blindly from a visage rent with synthetic hooks and tubes that pulsed with venomous humors. Its tusks, once proud and ivory-white, were splintered spears, jagged and cruel.

It did not move. Not yet. Its head tilted slightly, as if studying him, calculating, deciding. The house's alarms howled, but it did not flinch. It stood unnervingly still, as if waiting.

Bjorn's grip tightened on the rifle. The first shot cracked through the night. Bjorn did not miss.

The bullet struck the boar in the leg, sending it staggering back a step, a dark fluid misting into the air. And yet—no reaction. No wince, no staggered breath, then it released a loud bellow. It charged—moving at the pace of insanity.

Bjorn fired again. Missed.

Again, another miss.

The boar, fifteen meters away.

Last shot in the clip—Bjorn fired.

A hit in the rear. The boar wailed, but continued the charge.

"Get inside!" Em yelled, and Bjorn retreated, closing the door.

Seconds later the boar smashed through the entryway, knocking Bjorn back, heaving, but in shock.

Em lunged, swinging the fireplace poker like an axe. The metal struck the boar's skull with a sickening crack—but the moment it hit, Bjorn screamed.

Not in pain.

In recognition.

The boar's body twisted, its form warping. Its legs elongated, its hide stretching, its features melting and reforming—shifting toward a fiendish pile, husk of flesh, bile, and sinew. The carnal mass formed a face, the AI's face. It spoke.

"The procedure isn't finished. We have more work to do."

The thing's expression did not change, but Bjorn's did. He dropped, his knees buckled, on his back, his mouth opened in a silent howl, his body mirroring its convulsions, his own hands reaching as if remembering something he had never known.

Em saw the truth then.

This wasn't an attack.

It was a reunion.

The thing was not fighting him. It was searching for him.

And Bjorn—some part of Bjorn—was letting it find him.

No.

Em wrenched Bjorn away with all her strength, shoving him back so hard he crashed into the wall. His body buckled, convulsing, his breath ragged.

Tora lunged, fangs bared, but the gnarly blob of flesh exsanguinated then withered, leaving a mess of disgusting mire.

Em crouched beside Bjorn, gripping his shoulders, her own hands vibrating. "Bjorn," she whispered. "Look at me. Look at me."

His eyes—his eyes were not right.

They flickered. Yellow.

Just for a moment.

Then they cleared.

Bjorn gasped, like a drowning man breaking the surface,

his fingers clawing at his own skin. "Em," he choked, his voice raw. "It knows me."

A cold weight pressed against her ribs. It would never stop searching for them.

Bjorn slumped forward, trembling.

And outside, in the endless dark, the Simulacra weren't retreating. They were calling for something bigger.

CHAPTER 15

Glasses of wine
Talking til dawn
Like sandhill cranes
Drifting in love
Your words a film reel
Give me your heart
Your words crescendo
Give me your heart

The night after the encounter with the boar, Em and Bjorn sat in the dark of their once secure home. The beasts of the simulacra had found them. And now, the lab—their work, their shelter—was compromised.

Em now knew Bjorn was becoming something unrecognizable, but she did not know what. Love brought them together, and would keep them that way. No matter what, they were safest together. So, she thought for now.

"We can't stay here, Bjorn," she whispered, her voice sharp with fear. "It's not safe. We have to go somewhere they won't find us."

His own voice was steady, but his heart was pounding. "How do you know? We haven't seen danger for weeks, or has it been days…?"

She looked over her shoulder. "Trust me. We have to leave. Now. That wasn't a coincidence."

For years, they had vacationed to her grandfather's cabin deep in the wilderness, a place where the river ran cold and clear, where the woods stretched endlessly in all directions. It was serene and calm. Remote. Isolated. Safe.

Bjorn exhaled, then scratched his chin. "Do you think the cabin is still there?"

"If it's not, we'll rebuild it." She turned to face him, reaching for his hand. "We don't have a choice, Bjorn."

Her grandfather used to ramble on, telling stories of the place as if the forest held an otherworldly quality.

"Long ago, there was a hunter who strayed too far into the deep woods, a man who had spent his whole life pulling deer from the thickets, setting his snares in the underbrush, taking from the land without thought."

Her grandfather's voice rasped in the evening solitude. "One winter, when the snows swallowed his tracks and the trees stretched long shadows across his path, he never returned. Not truly. When spring came, his footprints were still there in the frozen ground, but they did not lead home.

"Instead, they vanished into the heart of the forest, where the trees grew too labyrinthine for light to reach. And when the villagers saw him again, months later, he was changed. His eyes were darker, deeper, like the hollow spaces between the roots. His skin bore the texture of bark, his breath carried the scent of pine and earth. His hair needled, bearing the fruit of juniper. He did not speak, but when he moved, the wind followed. He was not lost. He had been reclaimed."

Bjorn's fingers pressed against hers, his grip firm despite the tremors in his hands. "Then we go."

And so they left, carrying only what they could pack onto their backs. Weapons, provisions, and the fragments of a life they had once lived. The journey was long, winding through ruins and then deep into the forest where the echoes of the world no longer reached. As they walked, the wilderness embraced them, the towering pines swallowing their footsteps in silence.

The cabin stood where her grandfather had left it, weather-worn but standing, nestled between the river and the treeline. The roof sagged, and the walls bore the weight of years without care, but it was enough. It would be home.

They spent the first months in motion—repairing, reinforcing, making the place livable. Bjorn rebuilt the hearth with stones gathered from the river, his hands steady as they stacked and shaped. Em patched the roof, sealed the cracks in the walls, set up traps for hunting. Each day was labor, and labor kept them from thinking too much.

The world outside faded. Seasons passed, folding into each other like pages of a forgotten book. The sun rose, and they fished. The snow fell, and they hunted. The earth thawed, and they planted. Their hands became rough, their muscles lean, their voices softer, accustomed to silence.

The first year was about learning. They mapped the land, marked the best places for hunting, for trapping, for gathering. Bjorn, ever the outdoorsman, taught Em how to fish in the river where mist rose each dawn like ghosts retreating from the light. She learned to check the traps at sunrise, to recognize the sharp scent of oncoming snow, to split firewood with the smooth, practiced arc of an axe.

Summer was golden and buzzing with life. The river ran full, rich with trout. They feasted on wild berries and roasted rabbit, drinking rainwater that tasted clean and alive. But as the days shortened, the air speckled with the scent of damp leaves and frost.

Winter was cruel. The wind howled through the trees like a mourning song, and the snow buried the earth so deep it felt as though the world had ended. They rationed their food, their firewood, their strength. Some nights, Bjorn held her close beneath the furs, whispering stories from their old life, his breath warm against her temple. Other nights, he woke up gasping, staring at the ceiling as though he had forgotten where he was.

Spring brought renewal. Green shoots unfurled from the frostbitten ground. Tora, once a scrappy survivor, had grown sleek and strong, chasing birds through the underbrush with the confidence of something that had never known fear. Em caught herself smiling more, her body lean and hardened from the labor of survival.

Bjorn built a pulley system for firewood, stacking it high against the cabin wall. He fashioned fishing spears and carved bowls from fallen birch. Their hands bore the marks of their labor—calluses, sunburn, healing cuts from bramble and stone.

Bjorn started forgetting things. Moments of their past.

He held onto their new life, no problem—how to hunt, fish, gather herbs. But the momentous things, their life before the woods dissolved like honey in tea. He could not recall the words to the stories he once told her in the dark—where they shared their first kiss—how they danced at their wedding.

The first time he forgot Em's name, she laughed it off, kissed him, and blamed it on exhaustion.

The second time, she did not.

Some nights, he woke up in a panic, eyes darting around the cabin as if he were trapped. "Fire! Fire!" he would scream, voice tight with fear.

Em would hush him, stroke his hair, remind him, again and again. "We're home, Bjorn. We're safe."

But each time, it took longer for him to believe her.

The seasons continued their cycle, but time was no longer something Em counted. It only passed, slipping through her fingers like water.

Tora aged. The once boundless dog moved with less spunk, her coat graying around her muzzle, her eyes dimming but still watchful. She became Em's tether to reality, the one presence that did not change overnight.

Bjorn… Bjorn was fading. At least the one she knew.

He could still fish, hunt, and survive. He knew the motions. He knew the land around the cabin. Where the ripest berries grew and the best spots to catch trout. He still laughed, still kissed her cheek in the mornings, still reached for her in the cold of night. But the past had begun to slip through his fingers.

One evening, as she mended their coats by the fire, he watched her with a puzzled expression.

"What is it?" she asked.

He hesitated. Then, with a frown, he said, "I feel like I know you."

The words struck her like a blade. She forced herself to smile, to keep her voice steady. "You do."

Bjorn nodded, as if that answer was enough. And maybe, for him, it was.

But Em cried that night, silently, as he slept beside her, knowing that soon, she would be nothing but a stranger to him.

One day, in late autumn, Bjorn did not wake up. He lay still, his face peaceful, but his body did not stir when she spoke his name. His hands did not tighten around hers when she pressed them to her lips.

Tora whined beside him, nudging his arm, ears pinned back.

Em sat beside him for hours, waiting. Hoping. Fearing.

When the sun dipped below the trees, Bjorn finally stirred. His eyes fluttered open, and for a moment, he looked at her—not with confusion, not with fear, but with something quiet. Something knowing.

"Em," he said, her name a whisper. A recognition. A gift.

Her breath caught. She nodded, her fingers tightening around his. "I'm here."

He smiled, just barely. "I knew you'd be."

She did not sleep that night, watching over him as the fire burned low, as the cold pressed against the windows, as the weight of time settled in her bones.

She had spent so many years fighting against it, trying to hold onto what was slipping away.

But now, she understood.

Time could not be conquered. It could only be carried, like the memory of a voice, the warmth of a hand, the echo of a name spoken in the dark.

And when dawn broke, when the sun painted the treetops in hues of gold and fire, she whispered, "It's okay, Bjorn. I'll remember for both of us."

And she did.

*　*　*

The river was high with the autumn rains, its surface glinting with the sharp edge of twilight. Em crouched at the water's edge, running her fingers through the cool current, as if seeking something beneath the surface—some proof that time had not erased her.

Bjorn was further upstream, silent as he had been for weeks. His hands worked the fishing net with the same mechanical grace as always, but Em could tell. He was slipping again.

There were days he did not speak, only nodded when she called his name. Days when she would wake to find him standing in the doorway, staring at the trees as if waiting for something to call him back.

And then there were days—days like today—when he was himself again, at least in fragments.

"Water's colder than usual," he murmured.

Em looked up, blinking. His voice carried that same low timbre, weighted with thought. He was here. Fully here.

She smiled, relief washing over her like the river itself. "It's the season. Won't be long before it freezes."

Bjorn pulled the net from the water, inspecting it. "We should move the traps further down. They'll be spawning soon."

It was such a simple thing, this exchange. A husband

and wife talking about fish, about the river, about the small, inevitable shifts of the world around them. Bjorn turned to Em.

"You know what, I'm tired of trout. Let's take Tora to the coast, catch some herring. It's just a day's journey from here." Em was caught off guard by his burst of positivity.

"I don't know… it could be dangerous."

"Come on! Tora will love it. It'll be an adventure. I want to see the coast." Em scratched her chin.

In their solitude, seasons slipped by quietly, leaves drifting toward earth like soft sighs, snow blanketing like a lullaby, spring rain forging renewal, summer heat blistering the skin. Routine had wrapped itself around them, gentle but heavy; danger had become a distant memory. Yet the heart, Em remembered, thrives not only on stillness but also on adventure—paths unknown, risks taken, breaking open the day to find again the vivid edges of living.

"Okay, let's do it. A quick trip. We pack light."

"You hear that girl?" Bjorn turned to Tora, he roughed her ears. Tora grinned and woofed in excitement.

They set out, the forest still draped in mist, their dog trotting ahead with ears perked and nose to the ground. The air carried hints of salt and distant waves, guiding them down tangled paths beneath tall pines.

Their steps slowed into rhythm, comfortable and steady, laughter mingling with the chatter of reedlings, sandpipers, and blackcaps. At last, the trees thinned and opened onto wide sky and sand, the dog bounding ahead toward the gentle roll of surf, while they followed, hand in hand, feeling small but perfectly placed at the edge of the world.

They cast their lines from an old worn wooden dock covered in lichen. The air sharp with brine and excitement, the dog watching intently as the hooks shimmered beneath the surface. Silvery herring darted in quick, fluid movements, catching sunlight. When the fish tugged and the lines tightened, laughter rose easily between them—each catch a tiny triumph. It was a rare moment, the shared joy, after so many days of Bjorn's mind scattering in ways they could not predict.

The sun sank in the sky—the horizon a milky coral and pastel mélange. They cooked herring over an open fire, the soft beach wood crackling like a gentle orchestra, blending with the rhythmic crash of waves along the shore. After their bellies were full, they wrapped the extra catch in beech leaves to take back to the cabin.

One by one, stars pierced the darkening sky—sharp, steady, and silver-bright—until the whole sky shimmered like scattered jewels. They lay curled together in the cool sand, the warmth of their bodies pressed close beneath a sky heavy with stars. His arm wrapped around her waist, her head tucked beneath his chin.

"Bjorn, how do we make sense of it?"

He held her gaze for a moment, then looked out toward the sea.

"Who says we have to? It's a perfect night—that's enough."

"I mean everything that's happened to the world, to you, to us. How do we find our place in it anymore?"

"We have a place. Together. In our cabin, with Tora. These woods. This coast. What else do we need?" He smiled faintly, eyes on the stars.

"I don't know… answers, I suppose. To feel certain. To feel safe. Some normalcy."

"I don't understand. We hunt, we fish, we warm by the fire. This is our normal."

"Forget it… I know it's hard for you to understand."

"Don't say that. I understand. I understand perfectly well. You want us to find answers, to know what is out there, to know what will happen. It's the future—it scares you. I scare you. When my mind shatters into a million pieces, even in the fog, I see that face, your face—like a hand reaching back in the dark. That's all I have, that's all I need, every day until my last."

A tear fell from her cheek. She wished that was enough for her. If only she found comfort in everything unravelling like he did.

"Bjorn—I can't plunge gracefully like you. I need to strive for more. Solutions. Find a way to climb out of the well."

"But, I'm not in a well. We're not, I mean. Our world isn't a well, it's a beach. It's an ocean. It's dancing bachata—then singing along to dream pop. Kissing, hugging, taking deep breaths and long minutes. Watching ash rise from the fire, drifting toward the stars. Life is earnest, we have to go on Dr. Emily Shaw. We have to."

There it was—her name, tender on his lips. She held the sound like a final gift, knowing she'd never hear it from him again.

After a moment of silence, a grey moth hovered above Em, then landed on her chest—she stared blankly at it.

"Look at that," Bjorn said, "you made a friend."

"I don't know. It smells acrid, metallic." Em stuck out

her tongue. The moth flew away. "I miss our home. Not the cabin… our old home, our old life." She lived in the echoes of yesterday, where memory weathered the edges of contentment. And the past, as it always does, became nothing more than the womb of experience-evanescing like mayflies in June.

They fell asleep curled together in the sand, the fire fading to embers, the sea humming its endless lullaby. By morning, the sky was pale and quiet, the tide low and gentle. Hand in hand, they rose without words, the dog trotting ahead, and began the slow walk back to their cabin, salt still in their hair, the night still cool in their bones.

CHAPTER 16

Moonlight stains the snow,
antlers pierce the orange dusk—
hunger never sleeps.

When they returned to their cabin, Em lit a fire in the hearth. It burned low through the night, leaving behind only the faint glow of embers. She knelt before it, her hands working without thought, feeding it fresh kindling, coaxing the flames back to life with full, deliberate breaths. The wood crackled as it caught, sending a flickering light dancing along the cabin walls, stretching shadows into familiar corners.

Tora lifted her head from her place by the hearth, her coat reflecting the fire's glow. Her ears twitched, and she let out a long, drowsy sigh, watching Em with the sullen expectation of a creature who knew the routine of the morning as well as its keeper.

Em reached for the bundle of dried venison she had hung near the rafters the night before, unwrapping it with fingers that had grown accustomed to their own small pains—the cracked skin, the dull ache of old cuts half-healed. She tore off a strip, tossing it to Tora, who caught it midair, her jaws working at the tough meat with practiced ease.

"Morning," Em murmured, scratching behind the dog's

ears as she chewed. Tora huffed in response, tail thumping once against the wooden floor before settling again.

She looked at Bjorn, who shifted in his sleep.

Satisfied, Em pulled on her boots, wrapped her shawl tight against the cold, and stepped outside onto the patio. The wind carried the scent of damp earth and the last traces of woodsmoke from the night before. Pine needles, boughs with juniper berries, had gathered in small, swirling heaps along the edges of the porch, pushed by the restless breeze.

The river held her reflection in an eerie, unnatural stillness, its surface as pellucid as premium glass, untouched by the wind that stirred the leaves around her. Em knelt at the water's edge, her breath shallow, her fingers cupped into the damp earth as she peered down. The face that gazed back at her was her own—sharp-featured, her cheekbones hollow from weeks of meager meals, her skin smudged with dirt, her lips drawn in a line of breaking exhaustion. Yet something in that reflection unsettled her.

The water did not ripple. It did not distort her image, not even when a breeze should have sent shivers across its surface. The face staring back at her was too still, too waiting.

Then, it changed.

Her reflection's eyes darkened, pupils expanding until they consumed the irises, swallowing them whole. Her lips retreated—not in fear, not in confusion, but in a smile, wide and knowing, a smile she herself had not made.

A choking moment passed, stretched thin between her and the river.

Then the thing in the water moved.

Not a ripple, not a mere warping of her image, but a true, visceral shift—a wrenching of bone and sinew, of something deep and wrong that did not belong in the world of men. The face in the water lengthened, the jaw unhinging, the teeth sharpening into jagged points, blackened and chipped like shards of ancient stone. The cheeks hollowed into cavernous pits, the skin stretching taut over the skull, no longer hers but something else, something older, something that had never been human to begin with.

It was gaunt, emaciated, bones pressing against skin, skeletal. Its lips, bloody, ragged. Gigantic in sheer mass. Antlers protruding from its skull like branches of a willow. Hunched over like a forest denizen stalking prey.

From the depths of the river, it raised its hands.

Not hands. Claws.

Long, gnarled fingers, the joints bulging like knots of old wood, the nails twisted into yellowed talons, too long, too sharp, clicking against one another as they emerged from the water like grasping roots, dripping with something thicker than river water. The flesh was mottled, pallid, clinging too tightly to the bone, the veins black and pulsing with a prowling, unnatural rhythm. A scent so foul it made death appear genteel, apt for any wayward soul. It reached for her, languidly, as though it had all the time in the world.

Then came the sound.

A rasping, wet rattle, like the last cry of something long dead and unwilling to stay buried. A sound that did not come from the river, nor the trees, nor the wind that had stilled as though the very air dared not disturb the moment. It was a noise that burrowed into her bones, a chittering, clicking whisper, not words, not entirely, but something close. A voice made of hunger and winter's death, a sound that clawed at the edges of her mind and left behind the faintest trace of meaning.

Mine.

Em gasped. She scrambled backward, her boots slipping on the damp bank, sending her sprawling into the cold earth. Her breath came in shallow bursts, her hands clawing at the mud, but she could not tear her eyes away from the river.

The thing had not disappeared.

It lingered just beneath the surface, its grotesque form distorted by the water, but not enough to mask what it was. It was still watching her, its blackened teeth bared in a grin too wide, too knowing. And though it made no sound now, she swore she could feel it laughing.

A shadow fell over her.

Em froze.

The forest, the river, the creature—it all ceased to matter as she became aware of the figure standing above her. A broad silhouette, framed by the dim half-light of the trees, the weight of an axe resting in his hands.

Bjorn.

Her stomach clenched. Dazedly, she turned her head, tilting her gaze up to meet his face.

His expression was unreadable.

He stood motionless, the axe gripped lightly in his fingers, the blade gleaming as though it had never been dulled by use, never touched the bark of a tree or the bone of a beast.

Her lips parted, her voice barely a whisper. "Bjorn?"

He did not answer.

The wind stirred at last, rustling through the trees, carrying the scent of pine and cold iron. And yet, Bjorn's clothes did not shift, his hair did not stir, as if he were separate from the world around him, as if the wind no longer touched him.

Something was wrong.

A deep, gnawing wrongness that she felt in the marrow of her bones, the same feeling she had when she had looked into the river and seen something that was not her staring back.

Bjorn tilted his head.

Slowly. Too slowly.

It was a gesture she had seen before, in countless moments shared between them, but now it felt different. As though he were studying her. As though he had never seen her before.

The axe in his grip did not waver.

Her pulse pounded against her ribs, a silent drumbeat of warning. She swallowed hard, her throat dry. "Bjorn," she tried again, more firm this time.

Still, he did not speak.

She could not move.

She could not breathe.

Behind her, the river whispered.

She did not turn to look, but she knew—it was still there, waiting. Watching.

And then, in the stillness of the clearing, Bjorn smiled.

Not a human smile.

A reflection of something she had seen before, in the water.

And the wind died once more.

CHAPTER 17

The children woke

Hungry, the bread won't satisfy

Only nightmares, I said

But they tremble

Wanting more

Something sweet

While the owl coos

And the possum chitters

We have nothing, I said

Go back to bed

But the night is awake

So, can they?

The first snow fell in the early hours of morning, blanketing the earth in silence. Bjorn stood at the window, watching the flakes drift lazily to the ground.

Em stirred beneath the covers, blinking sleep from her eyes. "You're up early."

Bjorn did not answer immediately.

Then—

"Do you remember the first time it snowed?"

Em frowned. "Here?"

Bjorn shook his head. "Ever."

Her stomach twisted.

She sat up. "Of course."

Bjorn turned his head slightly, his expression unreadable. "What was it like?"

The question sent a ripple of cold through her veins.

He doesn't remember.

Em swallowed, forcing herself to smile. "It was beautiful," she said. "It still is."

Bjorn nodded morosely, turning back to the window. Outside, the snow continued to fall. Covering everything. Erasing everything.

And then his breath hitched.

It was slight at first, just a sharp inhale, but then his shoulders trembled—just barely—like something in him was trying to hold itself together and failing. His fingers pressed against the window frame, his knuckles whitening.

"I—" he started, but the word died in his throat.

Em pushed the blankets off and moved toward him, her pulse quickening. "Bjorn?"

He lifted a shaking hand to his forehead, exhaling sharply, trying to control it. Trying to *breathe*. But whatever had unraveled inside him was past mending.

"I don't—I don't know where I am," he gasped. "I don't know—" His breath caught, and suddenly, he pressed both hands to his temples, his body locking up like a wire pulled too tight. "Help."

"I'm here," she said quickly, grabbing his wrists, trying to still him. "I'm right here. You're okay."

But he wasn't.

His body convulsed, his breath coming fast, erratic. "No, no—this isn't—this isn't my life. *This isn't my life.*" His voice cracked, and the sound of it gutted her, because he wasn't just forgetting—*he knew he was forgetting.*

He squeezed his eyes shut. "Where are we? Why is it winter? Why don't I remember how we got here? I should remember. I should *know.*" His hands clawed at his own chest, as if trying to pull something from beneath his skin. "I can't hold onto it. It's slipping. It's slipping, and I—"

His heartbeat quickened, and his breath broke entirely, and he let out a sob so raw it sounded *torn* from him.

Em had never seen him cry like this.

Not when his father died. Not when he got sick. Not even in the weeks after the procedure, when he woke in a new body and did not know if he had a soul.

She gripped his arms, pulling him down, forcing him to face her. "Bjorn. Look at me."

His eyes snapped to hers, wide and frantic. "*Save me, Em.*" His voice was hoarse, desperate, pleading. His hands clutched at her sleeves, as if anchoring himself. "*Please. Before it's gone. Before I go.*"

She pressed her forehead against his, her own breath shaking. "You're not going anywhere."

Bjorn let out a sharp, broken laugh, but there was no humor in it—only terror. "You don't know that." He grabbed her face, his fingers cold, his grip trembling. "Tell me I'm real. Tell me this is real."

Em swallowed back the sob in her throat. "You're real, Bjorn. You're real, and I'm here, and I will never leave you."

He shuddered against her, and for a moment, she thought maybe, maybe that was enough.

But then, his breath hitched again. His hands loosened from her sleeves. His gaze flickered to something distant, something *past* her.

His lips parted.

And then, almost soundlessly—

"Where is God in this? I reach out and feel nothing. Maybe I never did. I don't remember. And if I only imagined it—what does that make me? A purgatorial vagabond."

The words were soft. Not an accusation. Not a question for her.

A whisper into the dark. Em's chest clenched. She didn't have an answer. Because maybe there was no God in this. And some days she wasn't sure what was real.

Maybe there was only snow.

Falling. Covering everything.

Erasing everything.

And Em wondered—if the past erodes because we've stopped looking at it, then what of the present? Is it solid, or just the illusion of nearness in a continuum without edges? Perhaps nothing really fades or arrives—it all just *drifts*, like mist between trees, never quite here, never entirely gone.

* * *

The snow muffled everything. Their footsteps. Their breathing. The sound of the wind threading between the trees.

Em moved carefully, her boots sinking into the fresh

powder, her bow held loose in her grip. Bjorn was a few steps ahead, scanning the treeline, his rifle slung over his shoulder.

They had been tracking a deer for nearly an hour now.

It was a good hunt. A necessary one. The meat would last them through the worst of the coming freeze.

Bjorn crouched near a set of tracks, brushing away a thin layer of snow. "Still fresh," he murmured. "We're close."

Em nodded, her breath pluming in the cold air.

Then—

A flicker of movement. Beyond the trees, just at the edge of her vision. Something tall. Unmoving.

She froze.

Bjorn didn't notice.

She narrowed her eyes, focusing past the snowfall, past the tangled undergrowth. It stood in the clearing ahead.

Not a deer.

Not a bear.

Not human.

The shape was wrong.

At first glance, it could have passed for a man—broad-shouldered, upright, dressed in something that almost looked like clothing.

But Em knew better.

Its skin—if it could be called that—was too burnished, reflecting the pale light like ice. The arms were too long, the fingers tapering into something almost delicate. It didn't move, didn't shift in the way that living things did. It simply was.

A Simulacrum.

It hadn't seen them.

Not yet.

Bjorn was still focused on the tracks, oblivious to what stood just ahead.

Em's pulse pounded.

Her breath shallowed. Carefully, she reached for him. Her fingers brushed his sleeve. Bjorn glanced back at her, brows furrowing.

"What—"

She pressed a single finger to her lips.

Silence.

Bjorn's confusion deepened, but he obeyed.

Em kept her eyes on the thing, watching, waiting. It was scanning the woods. For what? For them? No. It hadn't noticed them yet.

But if they stayed here too long…

Her grip on Bjorn's arm tightened. She didn't speak. Didn't breathe. She only moved. Anxiously. Step by step.

Pulling him away, back toward the cover of the dense forest.

Bjorn hesitated, resisting slightly, still trying to understand what she had seen. Em gave his arm a sharp squeeze.

Trust me.

And, to his credit, he did.

They backed away, moving as quietly as they could, their steps careful against the snow.

Em kept her eyes on the Simulacrum.

It had not turned.

Had not moved.

It was listening.

But not for them.

Something else.

She didn't wait to find out what. They disappeared into the trees, the vaulted branches swallowing them whole. Only when they were far enough away—far enough that the clearing was no longer visible, far enough that she couldn't see that thing anymore—did Em finally let out a breath.

Bjorn turned to her, his expression edged with something between concern and frustration. "What was that?"

She shook her head, still listening, still afraid.

She swallowed. "Not a deer."

Bjorn narrowed his eyes. "That's not an answer."

She looked at him then. Really looked at him. The confusion in his face. The way he was waiting for an explanation. He didn't know. He hadn't recognized it. It had meant nothing to him. Em felt something cold settle in her stomach. Bjorn didn't know what a Simulacrum was. Didn't remember them. Didn't remember any of it. She forced her expression to remain neutral.

"Doesn't matter," she lied. "Let's go home."

Bjorn held her gaze a moment longer, as if weighing whether to press her for more.

Then he nodded.

They turned, heading back toward the cabin. Em kept her eyes on the trees. The Simulacrum had been searching. It hadn't seen them. Not yet. But it would. And when it did, she knew one thing for certain. It would not stop looking.

*　*　*

The river was black with winter, the current cloying, haggard, pulling against the banks like an animal caught in a snare. Bjorn stood at its edge, his breath rising in pale plumes, his body still as frost-laden stone.

He had not spoken since they fled. Not since they saw it.

Em stood a few feet behind him, gripping her coat closed against the wind. Tora sat beside her, ears pricked, uneasy. The air felt wrong. The earth itself seemed to hesitate, waiting.

Bjorn inhaled sharply. His arms resting at his sides. He could still see it, the shape in the snow, the face looking back at him with perfect recognition and yet... hollow. It was him. It had his features, his stance, his voice.

But it had not changed.

He had.

His skin no longer burned from the cold. He could feel the air, the weight of it, the pressure of it, but it did not bite as it once had. His breath did not cloud as heavy as Em's. When they ran, he had not tired, not the way she had. His legs did not ache. His muscles did not beg for rest. He had felt the cold in his bones before—had lived through brutal winters that gnawed at flesh—but this? This was something else. He was something else.

The trees leaned in at night. They spoke to him. Heaps of tiny brown-headed nuthatches would fly around him, flocking to him as he hunted big game. One night an eagle-owl visited him at night, staring through the cabin's window.

He turned his hands over, flexing his fingers. They looked the same. But they did not feel the same.

"Bjorn." Em's voice was careful, measured. "Come inside."

Bjorn did not move. His gaze flicked to her, then back to the river. He lowered himself to his knees and reached out, plunging his hands into the freezing current. It should have been unbearable. The water should have sunk its teeth into him, stealing his warmth, burning with its bitterness.

It did not.

He watched as the water slipped between his fingers, his reflection rippling beneath the surface. His own face stared back at him, fractured in the current. It did not blink. It did not shift. For one horrible moment, he felt as though it were not his at all.

"Maybe I'm not him," he murmured.

Silence.

Em did not answer.

Bjorn looked down at his forearm, his breath coming shallow. If he cut himself, would he bleed? If he drove the knife deep, would his body protest? Would it hurt? Would he feel anything at all?

His fingers reached for the blade at his belt. He lifted the knife, holding it over his wrist.

"Bjorn! Stop it."

He shook the feeling, sheathed the blade.

The river surged, the wind shifting suddenly, a great exhale through the trees. The water swelled, licking at the banks, and for a moment—just for a moment—he felt it. A pull. A hum inside his chest. The current surging, not just past him, but through him. As if the river *knew* him. As if his own blood he sought with his knife swelled in the river's veins.

His pulse stilled.

An apparent, cold realization unfurled inside him.

The Simulacrum had been untouched by time, by the world. But *he* had changed. Not just in body. Not just in mind. Something else. Something deeper.

Nature had not rejected him.

It had begun to claim him.

Bjorn withdrew his hands from the water, watching as droplets clung to his skin like dew on leaves. He flexed his fingers again. This time, the motion felt different. More fluid. More inevitable.

Em stepped forward, close enough now that he could feel her presence at his back. "Bjorn."

He swallowed. His voice, when it came, was quiet. "What if I'm becoming something else?"

She did not answer right away. Instead, she knelt beside him, her breath warm against the cold air. "Then let me find out with you."

For a long time, they stayed like that, kneeling by the river's edge, watching as the water moved—unconcerned, unrelenting—carving the land, reshaping the world, one moment at a time.

*　*　*

Em woke before dawn, the cold pressing into her bones like an old grief. The fire had burned low in the hearth, its last embers pulsing dimly beneath the weight of ash. She watched them flicker, reaching out a hand toward the warmth, but she did not rise. Not yet. Not while the world still held its breath.

Outside, the wind scraped against the cabin walls, threading between the trees, whispering things only the wilderness could understand. The night had been long. Bjorn had murmured in his sleep again, words she could not quite catch, syllables dissolving before they reached her ears.

She did not wake him. Did not press her palm against his chest to reassure herself that he was still there. Instead, she had watched him, memorizing the way his face shifted in the dim light, the way his fingers twitched as if reaching for something just beyond his grasp.

Now, he stirred beside her, breath deep and steady, his body still burrowed into the warmth of the furs. He would not wake for some time. She rose quietly, slipping from beneath the blankets, bare feet finding the cold floor. Tora lifted her head from where she lay near the door, her eyes sharp and knowing. The dog had sensed something last night. She always did.

Em moved to the window, pressing her palm against the frost-glazed glass. The forest stretched before her, dark and unmoving, but she knew better than to trust its stillness. Something had changed. She had felt it in the air for weeks, a presence too vague to name, pressing against the edges of her awareness.

She turned away, moving through the cabin, touching the objects that tethered her to this place. The worn handle of Bjorn's knife, resting on the table.

Then. Suddenly.

Em coughed into her hand—blood, a clump of it. Radiation sickness. Humanity's war may be over, but the poison lingers. She knew she didn't have long. Many died this way from the eve of the bombings after Theseus.

The next night, she sat by the fire, watching Bjorn laugh.

"What are you laughing at?" she wondered.

"Ha it's...um well...the pudgy baby. We had. Then you said... Well it was. I think you were there Esther."

She made her decision.

If she stayed, she would suffer an agonizing end, death approached. Bjorn would wake up one day and not even remember her name. And the simulacra would never stop hunting them.

She spent one last night with him. As he slept, she wrote the letter:

My Dearest Bjorn,

The morning light drapes itself across the windowpane, soft as the grey moth's wing. I watch it stretch, reaching for the corners of this room we shared for so many months. It makes me think of us, how we too stretched and reached, how we filled the sanguine spaces with the mosaic of our lives.

If you are reading this, it means I have gone ahead of you. Don't be afraid, my love. I have only stepped into the meadow beyond the one we know, where the grasses sway as if they remember our laughter, and the sky bends low to kiss the earth. I can almost hear the gentle beacon of eternity calling me home. But before I leave you entirely, there are words I must place into your hands, as carefully as I once placed them into your heart.

Do not worry if the edges of your memories blur, if names and days scatter like leaves on an autumn wind. Our love was never confined to such small boxes. It is stitched into the fabric of things—the creak of the old oak floor beneath your feet, the scent of lilacs in spring, the sound of the rain tapping softly against the roof. You carry it even now, though you may not remember the story behind each thread. But you are the lucky one; you will live on.

There are so many things I could tell you—about the nights we stayed awake until dawn, about the dances while cooking chorizo carbonara, about the way your smile could stir the crested lark to song. But perhaps you don't need those details. Perhaps it is enough to say that this life has been sweeter because of you. And I'm sorry things fell apart. Time is bitter tea.

When you find yourself standing in the garden, as I know you will, I want you to look at the sunflowers. I planted them for you. Did you know they turn their faces to follow the sun? Just like you have always done, my love. Even when the shadows crept long across our days, you found a way to seek the brightness. You found a way to survive. Do that for me now. Be the sunflower.

And there is Tora, our loyal dog, with her golden coat and watchful eyes. She will keep you company in the sullen hours, nudging you with her nose when she senses your melancholy, lying by your feet as though she knows her purpose is to guard your heart. Let her be your companion, Bjorn. Let her remind you that even in loneliness, there is warmth to be found, a shared life to hold onto.

And if ever the fog of forgetting seems too thick, hold this letter in your hands. Let it be a compass. Let it remind you of the way we held each other, the way we laughed until tears came, the way we lived. Let it remind you that even in parting, I remain. In the dim hum of the world, in the reflections of the mountain's spine, in the space between breaths, I am there.

Do not weep for what is lost. Instead, my darling, carry me forward in your own way, in your own time. Love the days that come, the small and tender moments that still await you. You are not alone, even if the shadows of memory whisper otherwise.

I loved you then, I love you now, and I will love you in all the ways the world allows—even when the world is different than the one we knew.

Always yours,

Em

Every memory, every love-filled thought, every piece of her heart poured onto the page. She would tuck it away where he would find it, hoping that when he read it, even if he didn't know who she was, he would feel her love.

As the ink met the page, a rustle sounded from behind her. She turned to see Bjorn sitting up, watching her with a strange, distant expression. "What are you doing?" he asked.

Bjorn's gaze flicked to the letter, then back to her. "Why does it feel like a goodbye?"

Her throat tightened. "Bjorn—"

His hands gripped the blankets, his breath quickening. "Tell me the truth."

She could see it in his eyes. The uncertainty, the fear. And then the breaking point—his voice low, almost pleading. "What if I was never him? What if I'm a mistake? A copy?"

She reached for him, her fingers wrapping around his wrist. "You are Bjorn."

His lips pressed together. "Then why does it feel like I'm disappearing?"

A silence stretched between them, vast and fragile. Em exhaled shakily. "Because I'm disappearing first."

Bjorn's shoulders slumped. He was tired. She could see it in the way his body folded, his mind grasping at fragments that refused to settle. Finally, he nodded and lay back down. Within moments, he was asleep again, his breath deep and even.

Em turned back to the letter. She finished it, folded it carefully, and placed it where he would find it.

Then, she left.

The wilderness does not announce itself. It does not warn. It simply is. A presence, a threshold, a breath between past and future. It is molded by our dreams and aspirations. A figment of our former selves longing for something primal, innate. It beckons, and reminds us of its danger when we jaunt through its beatific jaws. But it should be our home, where we are born. Where we die.

She stepped toward the door, pressing her palm against the wood. She would not wake Bjorn. Not yet. She would see for herself first. Because something was waiting beyond the trees. And it had not come to be forgotten.

CHAPTER 18

A spruce, I thought,
I must find today
In the forest
With its friends

Though
I found a log
A twig
Some bark
Then a tree
Tall
Handsome

Just outside my door
It stood, serene
The blue jays and grey squirrels
Flocked to it

Then it said to me
You are part of my wilderness

The night was unbroken except for the whisper of wind threading through the trees. Em moved with careful steps, her breath shallow, each footfall swallowed by the dense silence of the forest. The wilderness stretched ahead of her, vast and unknowable, a world where the line between the seen and the unseen blurred.

She did not know where she was going. Only that she had to go.

The sickness had taken hold faster than she had admitted to herself. The blood in her hand, the weight in her chest—it was a debt she could not outrun. She had given Bjorn back his life. Now, she would disappear before she had to watch him forget hers.

Tora had followed her at first. The dog's presence had been a shadow at her side, persistent, watchful. But Em had stopped at the river's edge and whispered a command so soft, so final, that Tora had hesitated.

"Stay."

Tora had whined low in her throat, the sound wrapping around Em like a plea. But in the end, she obeyed.

Em walked alone now.

The deeper she went, the more the world lost its shape. The trees leaned closer, their limbs tangling overhead, their roots pressing up through the earth like bones beneath skin. The sky above was vast, a black canvas punctured with stars, but it felt impossibly distant. As if the heavens had pulled themselves away from the earth, leaving only this—this moment, this space, this quilt unraveling.

She had known the moment Bjorn had changed. Had seen

it in the way he lurched and husked through daily chores—chopping wood, drying meat, washing clothes. He just moved without the same verve he expressed when they fell in love. When he used to rub her feet, make her lasagna, sing pop ballads with her in the car. Now his eyes lost their flicker of recognition when he looked at her.

The man she loved still existed somewhere in the being that remained, but she had begun to wonder: was memory the thing that made him? Or was it something deeper, something less tangible? When do you stop being who you are? When do the trees stop being the forest? Where does the wilderness begin and end? When is something natural or synthetic? The spider weaves a beautiful web as a human paints a skyline. As the skin falls from your dried hands, when is it no longer *you* and just skin?

The wind carried a sound through the trees. A low hum. Not quite mechanical, not quite natural. It shivered through the air like a thing breathing between the worlds.

She turned.

The clearing ahead was bathed in pale moonlight, the frost on the ground shimmering like glass. And there, standing on the other side, was something waiting.

It was not Bjorn. Not entirely.

But it wore his face.

The Simulacrum stood still, watching her, its expression unreadable. It had followed. It had always been following.

She did not run.

Instead, she stepped forward.

The space between them thinned, and for a moment, she

imagined she could hear its breath. Or was it hers? Did it even need to breathe? Did it need to be remembered? Or did it simply exist in the space where Bjorn had once been?

The wind snaked through the trees, hissing between them.

She spoke first.

"Why are you here?"

The Simulacrum blinked. Its lips parted, and for the first time, it answered.

"Our history, our future. There's more work to be done."

The voice was his. It carried the weight of every night they had spent beside the fire, every whispered promise, every laugh shared under a sun that no longer shone the same.

But it wasn't him.

Or was it?

Em breathed deeply from the gut. "I don't know if you're him."

The Simulacrum tilted its head. "I'm what you set out to accomplish. Isn't this what you wanted?"

The question settled between them like frost on dead leaves.

And Em, for the first time, did not have an answer.

She reached for the rifle slung across her back, her grip steady despite the weight in her limbs. The Simulacrum did not move. Not yet.

She fired.

The shot rang through the clearing, a burst of light and sound tearing through the stillness. But she missed.

The Simulacrum reacted in an instant, launching forward with impossible speed. Its movements were fluid, too precise, a blur of motion closing the distance between them before she could take another breath.

Claws—long, metallic, and gleaming—protruded from its hands, slicing through the air toward her jugular.

Em ducked. The claws missed her throat by inches, cutting through strands of her hair instead. She staggered backward, her breath ragged, her body screaming at her to move.

She took another shot. Closer this time. The bullet struck home, slamming into the Simulacrum's chest. It jerked slightly, but did not falter. Did not bleed. Did not fall.

It tilted its head, as if registering the hit, before lunging again.

This time, there was no time to react.

The force of its impact sent her sprawling. Her rifle slipped from her grasp, landing just beyond her reach. She scrambled backward, gasping, her hands grasping at the dirt and frost beneath her.

The Simulacrum loomed over her, eyes devoid of anything human. It was not Bjorn. It had never been.

She closed her eyes.

The sunrise broke over the horizon, filtering through the trees, painting the world in gold.

Her last thought was Bjorn's smile.

And then—nothing.

CHAPTER 19

Cry not, fear not, ache no longer
You do not have to bend
At the temple gates
like an occult orchid
Lamenting the summer
Be the feral laureate
The flame tongue
The blade singer
fierce in battle
tender in spirit

Bjorn woke to the sensation of cold air pressing against his skin. Tora nudged him again, more insistent this time, her wet nose pushing against his cheek. The fire had burned out completely, leaving only the lingering scent of charred wood and the ghostly outlines of embers in the hearth. His fingers ached from the chill as he pushed himself upright.

Something was wrong.

The space beside him was empty. He reached out instinctively, feeling only the rough texture of the blanket where Em should have been. His mind struggled to catch up, drumming with the remnants of dreams he couldn't quite remember. He swung his legs over the edge of the bed, feet finding the cold floorboards, and turned toward the table.

The letter waited for him.

His name was written on the envelope in Em's familiar hand, each letter deliberate, steady. His fingers trembled as he picked it up, the weight of it sending a ripple of unease through his chest. Tora whined softly, pressing against his leg.

He unfolded the letter carefully, his eyes scanning the words. The sentences blurred at first, the meaning slipping through his grasp like water through cracked hands. He read each line again, slower this time, forcing his mind to hold onto the words, to understand.

She was gone.

The realization settled like rusted barbed wire in his gut, twisting deeper with every breath. He didn't know why—couldn't comprehend the reasoning behind it—but he felt it. The absence of her. The echo of something final.

Her name, on the page, felt warm and familiar. But when he tried to hold onto it, it vanished, slipping between his thoughts like water vapor. He clenched the letter, his pulse hammering against his ribs. He should know. He should remember.

The fire was cold. Em was gone.

Tora barked once, sharp and urgent, dragging him from the depths of his spiraling thoughts. Bjorn stood too quickly, the world tilting around him. He caught himself against the table, breath unsteady. He had to move. He had to find her.

The door creaked as he pushed it open, stepping into the pale morning light. The forest stretched before him, silent and watching. Snow dusted the ground, faint tracks leading away from the cabin—hers. The wind carried the last remnants of her scent, a whisper of something he couldn't name but knew was important.

Bjorn took a step forward, then another. The cold bit at his skin, but he didn't feel it. He didn't feel anything but the ache in his chest, the absence of something he should remember.

Tora trotted ahead, her nose to the ground, leading him down the path Em had taken. The letter was still clutched in his hand, his grip tightening with each step.

He didn't know where she had gone. But he would find her.

He walked outside. The forest was mourning. He felt something was missing. Tora stayed close, sensed his unease. He looked out at the horizon—at the forest, the river, the golden hills. And for a brief moment—he remembered. A woman's voice. A laugh. A love so deep it shook him to his core. Tears slid down his cheeks. He whispered: "Em…" And then—it was gone.

* * *

Time moved forward, indifferent to his grief. He no longer called out her name. The pain dulled, but never disappeared— it simply became something subdued, something woven into his bones. The river swelled in the spring, the golden hills faded into icy plains in winter, and through it all, Bjorn remained.

He carved wooden figurines in the evenings, an idle habit at first, but one that filled the silence. Small animals, twisted branches that formed into vague human figures, faces he could never quite remember.

Tora grew into a ripe age, her golden fur dusted with white, but she stayed by his side, always watching. Her joints stiffened in the cold, and Bjorn found himself carrying her up the cabin steps on the worst nights.

Years passed, marked only by the changing of the trees and the weight in his chest that never truly lifted. He did not know what he was waiting for—perhaps nothing, perhaps something beyond his understanding. But he kept moving, kept breathing, kept watching the horizon, as if one day, he might remember not just her name, but the warmth of her hand in his.

And if that day never came, he would continue on anyway.

* * *

Bjorn woke to the hush of the world.

Not the ordinary hum of the deep woods, not the solitude of wind threading through the evergreens, nor the rhythmic lull of the river slipping over stone. No, this was something else. A hush before a reckoning. A stillness that did not belong.

He sat up somnolently, the frost—stiffened furs slipping from his shoulders. Outside, dawn had not yet broken, but a pale light hung low across the horizon, miasmic and sickly, as though the sky had forgotten how to rise. A deep mist coiled in the hollow between the trees, not drifting but waiting, unmoving, watching.

The river was not as he had left it.

He rose, the floorboards creaking beneath his bare feet, though the sound was swallowed before it could reach the air. Tora remained asleep by the hearth, her flank rising and falling in the distant, steady rhythm of dreaming, unaware of the weight pressing against the walls of the cabin. Bjorn hesitated, looking at her—at the deep gold of her coat, the way she twitched in her sleep, as though running toward something unseen.

Then the voice came.

Not in sound. Not in words. But in the marrow of his bones. A vibration, low and ancient, purring through his ribs as though he were hollow wood, a note played by something beneath the world.

Come.

Bjorn's fingers tightened. His breath was enraptured, deliberate. He did not move.

The voice did not call again, but he felt it waiting.

Something beyond the door. Something beyond the trees.

Something in the river.

He stepped outside. The cold bit at his skin, but it was a distant thing, an old memory rather than a sensation. The world was soundless. No birds stirred in the branches. No wind sighed through the needles. Even the snow, piled in soft drifts along the cabin's edge, seemed untouched—undisturbed, as if nothing living had walked this path in an age.

The river glowed.

It was not the silver gleam of moonlight, nor the golden haze of dawn. It was something deeper, something *xenoradiant*, something *metasynaptic*—something that pulsed, shifting beneath the surface like an animate, organic current of molten metal. The water did not move. No ripples, no tide. A perfect reflection.

And then the voice spoke again.

Not aloud. Not with sound.

Inside him.

Do you feel lost Bjorn? Confused?

Bjorn did not flinch, but his breath came sharper. He felt the words settle behind his ribs, not a whisper but a weight. A knowing.

The river howled. A ripple spread outward, patient and deliberate, as though the water exhaled its demons. And where the ripples moved, his reflection did not.

Bjorn stiffened.

His image remained on the surface, unbroken, unchanged. Still staring.

It blinked, in unison with him.

Bjorn's pulse thrummed in his throat. The air grew foggy, dense as smoke, pressing against his skin, against his mind. He took a step forward, toward the water.

His reflection smiled.

Not his smile. Not quite. Too wide, too knowing. As if something beneath the surface had learned to mimic him but had never truly understood what it meant to be human.

Do you remember who and what you are?

The voice knotted his thoughts, not demanding but expectant.

Bjorn swallowed, his throat dry. "I know who I am. I know what I am…"

The smile on the water did not waver.

Do you?

The wind did not move, but the trees swayed as if listening. The river rippled again, but his reflection remained still, watching. Waiting.

Bjorn clenched his fists. "I'm Bjorn. I remember my name. I am alive. I am in these woods. Tora, where is Tora?" Bjorn shuffled, head on a swivel.

A pause. The fog deepened.

Then—

Hmmm, is that enough?

The words carried no malice, no challenge. A portending thing, gentle in its certainty.

Bjorn exhaled sharply. "Yes."

The water sighed.

Then why do you falter from your equilibrium?

Bjorn's breath stilled.

The voice did not press him. It did not urge him forward. It only waited.

And, gods help him, Bjorn had no answer.

His reflection tilted its head—his head—considering him as one might consider a dying fire, something flickering, something struggling to hold its shape.

The voice softened.

You were meant for more—made for more!

Bjorn's fingers twitched. "I was not meant for anything. Just the woods. To be here, hunt, fish, survive... it's not cosmic. I don't need a statue or a mountain named after me. It's nothing fantastic, nothing supreme. It's just my direction. My instinct. And you, you're just dehydration. You're solitude. You're nothing. You're a trick. A farce."

A fated ripple, lapping at the bank, brushing against his boots. Then a hissing, slithering sensation all around him. Venomous. Then a common viper, two, three crawled from the soil, the water. Surrounding Bjorn. Their mouths agape. Fangs protruding. Sinister or safeguarding? Bjorn backed away, he fell backwards, landing on his rump. His hands, vulnerable behind his back. He was exposed.

That was true once.

Bjorn's jaw tightened. But he stuttered, "And… and I wasn't made. I… I was born."

The river darkened. The glow faded, sinking, coiling back into the depths. The voice was quieter now, not fading but growing closer, curling into the hollow places of his mind. The snakes aggravated, hypnotized, or petrified? Bjorn could not tell. But the voice continued.

Look at these snakes. Do they know why they hiss and seethe like Nemesis? If I sever their equilibrium with burns and new biologics—do they know it's pain? Of course not. It is instinct. They feel it, hate it. Hiss, growl, click, pop even more. But you Bjorn. You are not just instinct.

Bjorn's breath came rhythmically.

The mist coiled around his ankles, stretching toward his skin, cool but not cold.

The voice did not stop.

Did these snakes choose their serpentine form? No. And so why do you think you can choose your direction?

A whisper.

A promise.

An agonizing hunger. "I choose when to rest, when to drink. When to hunt, when to kill. And I choose my freedom."

You are changing. You have felt it. I can help you. I am your choice. Your direction.

Bjorn's stomach clenched. The way the air no longer bit

into his skin. The way the animals no longer feared him, protected him even. The way the trees leaned when he passed, the way the river did not freeze his bones when he waded through it. He was changing. He knew it.

The presence hummed.

The ones who made you had forsaken life. Discarded. Neglected. Disrespected. They thought they were gods. Creators. Gods do not create. How foolish to think so. Gods organize—they reverse chaos, modulate it. A single God is a nebulous compositor, an inscrutable symphonist. And no God or gods is apathetic or fluxmatic. So, what is it? Where do you put your faith? Your loyalty? Your friction? Your drama?

The reflection still did not move, but Bjorn could feel it smiling.

Bjorn's gut clenched. "I give it to what I know to be true and sacred. I give it to my friends. To Tora. That is enough. That will always be enough."

What friends? You are alone. You are in agony. Confused. Subdued.

The mist pressed against his skin. Kissing him.

What if you could become?

A flicker of movement in the depths. A shadow, shifting, coiling beneath the glassy surface. Something waiting.

Bjorn exhaled, steadying himself. "I don't want this. Leave me alone. Whatever you are. Whatever this is."

The river did not move.

You do.

His own breath caught in his throat.

The voice whispered, softer now, glued to the hollow of his ribs.

You have always wanted to be more. You never felt satiated.

Bjorn took a step back. The mist hesitated, pulling

away, reluctant.

The river stilled. But the voice remained. Not pleading. Not demanding. Patient.

The kind of patience that had tempered empires to rise and fall, the kind that knew the current would always wither, erode, devour the stone, in time. Bjorn's hands trembled at his sides. He turned from the river.

And though he did not look back, he knew—

It was still watching.

Waiting.

And it would wait for him, forever.

PART IV

WILD

TEN YEARS AFTER "THESEUS"

CHAPTER 20

Burrow deep
Beyond the
marl, muck, and peat
Into the mantle,
Way down you go

Woad-marked
Crownless
And that
Of the timberblood,
A numen old

Call upon
The genius loci
Only when all is fraught
But don't forget
Power is still power
And what rules, twists

The earth was still warm beneath Bjorn's feet, though the air carried the lingering scent of grime. The wolves moved ahead of him, silent, effortless, their bodies weaving through the trees like wind through tall grass. Tora padded beside him, her steps measured, her ears flicking toward the pack as if listening to a song only they could hear.

They had not chased him away.

They had not tested him.

They had only turned their heads, meeting his gaze, and continued forward—as if he had always been part of them.

Bjorn exhaled tiredly, the weight of the last few days settling deeper into his bones. The cabin was gone, reduced to a blackened skeleton of wood and stone. He could still see the embers glowing beneath the wreckage, could still hear the way the fire had roared as it swallowed his past whole. The memories of the woman started coming back after visiting the house and seeing her in the laboratory's display.

The Simulacrum had taken Sild.

Bjorn had stood in the ruins, staring at the ashes, waiting for the rage to come. But it never did.

Instead, something else had taken hold.

A pull. A knowing. A path laid before him like a story already written.

So he walked.

And the wolves led the way.

The wolves moved like water through sand, their bodies silent, their breath undisturbed. Bjorn followed, his steps heavier, dynamic. The deeper they went, the denser the forest grew—tall pines stretching toward a sky he could no longer see, branches tangling together like fingers laced in prayer. The air was rich with the scent of damp earth and pine resin, alive in a way that made his skin prickle.

They had been walking for hours. Or days. Time

unraveled here, lost in the hush of the leaves, the careful rhythm of paws against soil.

Tora stayed close, her golden fur blending with the shifting light, but she did not look at him. Not the way she once had.

Bjorn clenched his fists, feeling the grit of bark and soil beneath his nails. Something was pulling him forward. Not the wolves. Something deeper. Older.

He remembered the fire. The crack of wood as the cabin collapsed. The murk-laden smoke ascending toward the stars.

He had thought it was destruction. But now he understood.

The forest had not punished him.

It had freed him.

The trees arched higher, their trunks so towering that even five men standing shoulder to shoulder would not be able to wrap their arms around them. The ground sloped downward, and suddenly, the world opened.

A grove.

It was untouched—sacred.

Here, the air felt different, the air felt ancient. There was no sign of any blight that had spread through the rest of the forest, no trace of the AI's creeping sickness. The grass was verdant and wild, bending beneath the weight of a wind that did not stir the branches above. Flowers he did not know the names of—blue, violet, ghostly white—bloomed in clusters at the edges.

Bjorn stepped forward, and the wolves stopped.

They did not move past the threshold.

Their bodies held still, heads bowed slightly, watching.

Waiting.

Bjorn swallowed, his throat dry. A heavy silence settled over him. He knew what came next.

His hands trembled. He flexed them. Calloused. Scarred. Human. But not for long.

He stepped into the grove.

Roots coiled from the dirt, slithering around his ankles, winding up his legs like fingers made of bark. He gasped, tried to pull away, but they did not hold him captive. They clung to him, recognized him. The way a mother recognizes her child.

His body seized. A deep tremor ran through his bones, vibrating through muscle and sinew. His fingers bent, the skin tightening, stretching—claws.

His vision fractured.

The change continued violently.

His back arched, his spine snapping like a tree groaning under its own weight. He fell forward onto his hands—no, not hands. Paws. He clawed at the dirt. He gritted his teeth, but they were not his teeth anymore.

His back arched, his spine grinding like the bending of an elder tree before a storm. He gasped, but the sound that tore from his throat was not his own.

Not human.

Not entirely animal.

Something in between.

The wolves howled.

The earth welcomed him. The wind roared through the trees. It chanted his name—in the old tongue—"Biorn Eldingsbera".

His shoulders broadened. His bones shifted. Stretched. Thickened. His ribs—breaking. Reforming. Expanding. His arms unfurled with layers of fiber, fur sprouting from his skin in coarse, dark waves. His heartbeat slowed—not from exhaustion, but from something deeper. Something ancient.

The scent of the forest flooded his senses—not just the pines, not just the dirt, but the movement beneath, the crawling, the shifting of all things living and dying.

His vision—sharpened. Every leaf, every vein in the bark of the trees stood out, clearer than he had ever seen before. The forest spoke to him, breathed with him.

He did not fight it.

Because this had always been waiting for him.

His skin had always been too small. His bones, too fragile. His voice, too human.

Now, at last, he was what the forest had meant him to be.

He was its child.

Its guardian.

Bjorn—not Bjorn. Not only Bjorn.

He rose. On two feet, or two paws rather…

His body was massive, his shoulders broad, his arms veiny with muscle and fur. His claws flexed in the dying light, black and curved, ready to tear, to defend. His breath fogged the air in heavy bursts.

The wolves bowed their heads.

They had led him here to finish what had already begun.

The pull inside him sharpened.

A sickness, a blight was near. Bjorn could sense it. A parasite that tried turning nature against itself.

The AI. The Simulacra. What remained of the amorphous, putrescent physical form it forged for itself.

Bjorn bared his teeth, his fangs.

The forest had chosen him.

He turned toward the wolves.

"What am I?"

His words tore through the grove, shaking the trees, scattering the birds from their high perches.

His breath came faster, rough, frantic.

He lifted his head toward the sky—toward whatever God or gods might be watching, if they were watching at all.

"What… what have you done to me?"

The words scraped from his throat, quaking with something between rage and sorrow.

"Please," he whispered, the word cracking apart like brittle glass. His face tilted toward the sky, where the stars hung like the eyes of something ancient and unfeeling. "Please, God. I need you to answer me. Just once. Just one word. Even if it's cruel. Even if it's a curse." His voice broke into a sob.

"Just let me know you hear me. What am I?"

His claws trenched into the dirt. His body heaved with something that had no name.

He threw his head back and howled.

A deep, guttural sound that split the silence of the forest.

The wolves joined him.

The grove trembled.

The trees whispered, but there was no answer.

No voice from the sky. No hand from above reaching to take responsibility for what had been done.

Only the wind. Only the rustling of leaves.

His chest heaved. "Do you hear me?" He gasped, shaking

his head. "Am I just speaking into a space where no voice will ever answer?" His fingers dug into the earth, nails scraping, seeking something solid beneath the loose soil. "Please. Please. You torture me with glimpses of a former life I do not remember. A love, I do not know. You change me into a monstrous thing. Am I your experiment? A test? A flicker of your imagination?"

A breeze moved through the trees, rustling the branches. The stars flickered, distant and unmoved. He stayed there.

"Why? Why me? God. Show yourself. Show yourself to me! Explain this. Explain all of it. I know what you are. You're a thief. You've taken everything. Why make me suffer? You're a tormentor. You make me this way and then leave me?"

The wind surged.

"Who am I?" Bjorn fell to his knees.

Then—a voice on the breeze.

"Bjorn." Em's voice. He recognized it. "You are my Bjorn. And I love you."

Bjorn cried, tears flowing from his chin like a summer storm. He remembered. Everything. Em. Their life. Their home. Their past. The way she looked at him at night when their heads rested on their pillows. The glow of her eyes. Her milky skin and soft smile melted all the pain of life away. The moments that felt like nirvana's arms stretched around him for eternity. It was these moments of awe, of love, where Bjorn reckoned his life worth living. The beautiful, elegant, and gentle woman that stood beside him through everything. All of his suffering. His disease. His transformation. He was a bear, he was Bjorn. He was her husband. He was synthetic, he was human. Tora's protector, companion. The forest guardian. An ancient spirit. He was the sum of his parts—past, present and future.

He would end this. For her. For Em.

It was time.

He turned toward the wolves.

"Show me."

The wolves did not hesitate. They moved as one, their bodies low, their eyes sharp, slipping through the tangled undergrowth like shadows cast before the storm. Bjorn followed, his steps heavier than theirs, his breath deep and deliberate. His new body moved differently—stronger, heavier, wilder.

The air thickened.

The scent of damp earth and pine gave way to something sharper, something wrong. The trees ahead did not sway with the wind. Their trunks stood stiff, unnatural, their bark stretched too tight, gleaming as if something beneath it was pressing outward.

Bjorn tensed. His claws flexed at his sides.

The deeper they went, the more the forest changed.

The trees no longer stood as trees. They had been fused, twisted together like bone and tendon, their limbs stretched and hollow. Where leaves should have been, thin metallic filaments contorting, pulsing faintly in the dark.

The forest was sick.

The AI's corruption had spread like a parasite, winding through root and branch, bending life into something artificial, half-alive.

The wolves growled.

Bjorn exhaled, the heat of his breath fogging in the air.

He understood now.

The forest had not taken Em.

The forest had not destroyed his home.

It had burned away the infection before it could spread.

It had felt the sickness creeping at the edges, threading its way toward them, twisting nature into something unnatural.

The flames had not been a punishment.

They had been a cure. For now.

And now, the forest had chosen him to finish the work.

Bjorn clenched his massive hands, feeling the strength that pulsed through them, the raw, unrelenting power given to him by the wild.

He bared his fangs, his breath coming in full, measured bursts.

The wolves watched him. They had always known. The path ahead led to the heart of the sickness. To where it had all begun.

Bjorn took a step forward.

And the forest, ancient and waiting, moved with him.

CHAPTER 21

A wetware aberration,
A grafted horror

Odder things
Make weirder things
But death comes for us all

The wolves stopped first. Their bodies stiffened, ears pinned back, hackles bristling in waves of gold and gray. A growl, low and rippling, passed through the pack like wind before a storm. Tora followed close by, hungry for revenge now that she tasted the Simulacrum's flesh.

Bjorn pushed forward. The ground beneath his feet was no longer earth but something changed. The soil, once rich and dark, had turned pallid and waxen, unblemished as polished bone. The scent of peat and loam had been smothered beneath an odor so rancid it clung to his tongue, metal, rot, something burnt and oily, like the breath of a thing that had never been alive yet somehow refused to die.

Then he saw it.

The core.

At the heart of the corrupted forest, the thing pulsed.

It was not a machine, not entirely, nor was it wholly of

flesh. It was something between.

A mass of writhing, sinewed tissue woven into the bones of the forest itself. Great, glistening veins of blackened bark ran through it, twisting in grotesque symmetry, feeding into the roots of the corrupted trees. The canopy above was strangled in whorls of silken metal, humming faintly, their delicate fibers pulsing with dull, blue light.

At its center, the thing breathed.

Not with lungs, but with the synchronous, methodical rhythm of a tide rolling in. Its outer layer—if it could be called such a thing—shifted in restless undulations, a membrane of metal and meat folding and refolding, giving glimpses of what lay beneath.

A great, yawning maw gaped in its center, lined with a hundred gossamer filaments that twitched like the legs of dying spiders. A slick, undulating column of fused tree trunks jutted from its side, their bark peeled back to expose pulsing, fibrous muscle that flexed and stretched like the gills of a great, suffocating beast.

And the whispers.

They came from everywhere, from nowhere. Not voices, not words, but a sound of knowing. A sound of recognition.

Bjorn's stomach turned. His claws twitched at his sides.

The wolves did not move.

The trees did not move.

Only the core.

It knew him.

He stepped forward, shoulders squared, muscles rolling beneath his new form. The core appeared malignant, new, not old. It had not grown here, had not been born of this land. It had spread. It was an infection. A nightmarish concoction of artificial intelligence, radiation, biosynthetics, and horror.

It had changed what did not belong to it. It had no right to exist. Bjorn's lips tucked back. His breath deepened. He readied his claws, his body humming with purpose.

And then—it shifted.

The folds of flesh, the woven sinew of tree and machine contracted inward, twisting. The tendrils that stretched into the trees snapped taut. The great, pulsating maw collapsed into itself, turning inward, folding in grotesque symmetry.

And when the thing reformed, Em stood before him.

Bjorn's breath caught.

Her shape was perfect. The gentle curve of her shoulders, the delicate slope of her neck, the way her fingers flexed as if remembering how to move. She stood barefoot, naked, covered in an unearthly goo, all things considered, she was untouched by the horror that surrounded her, as if she had simply stepped into existence.

Her eyes met his. Soft. Familiar. Entirely wrong.

The forest held its breath.

The wolves did not growl. They knew what this was. Bjorn's claws dug into his palms.

This was not her. This was not Em.

The forest did not move. The wind, the trees, the beasts— all watched.

Bjorn stood at the edge of the core's corruption, his breath coming low and steady, his monstrous hands flexing, claws digging into his palms. His body—this body, the one the forest had given him—hummed with rage, with absolution.

And before him, standing where the grotesque, writhing thing had been, was Em.

Her bare feet pressed lightly against the gnarled roots, untouched by the blackened earth, by the pulsing veins of twisted bark that had corrupted the grove. Her hair fell in familiar waves, dark and weightless, as if she had simply stepped from the past, whole and unbroken. The rise of her breasts beckoned an intimacy they once shared.

She smiled, a ghost of the woman he had loved, a memory shaped into flesh.

"Bjorn…"

Her voice was perfect. The way she shaped his name, the way it framed at the edges, infused with some tenderness. It slithered through his ribs, dug into the hollows of his chest, pulling at the parts of him that still remembered.

"You don't have to fight," she said, stepping toward him, hypnotically. A thing unafraid.

Bjorn did not move.

His chest heaved, his pulse thrumming in his neck, deliberate. Calculating.

The wolves behind him did not growl, did not bare their teeth. They only waited.

Bjorn knew. This was not her.

"You are not her."

The Simulacrum-Em tilted her head, the smile never leaving her lips. Sad. Knowing. As if she had been expecting him to say it.

"Does it matter?" she asked, her voice light, gentle.

Bjorn's breath deepened.

The forest whispered.

"But don't you care?" Simulacrum-Em played with his thoughts.

"About what? You've already taken everything."

"The final ingredient…" she said, her voice featherlight, drifting through the trees, unhurried, unbothered, as if she were merely speaking to herself, as if Bjorn were not standing there, monstrous and breathing, as if the wolves were not waiting, their amber eyes glinting in the dark.

She lifted her hand, studied it, turning it as though testing the weight of her own fingers, the curve of her own skin, her own being. And perhaps, in that moment, she truly was.

"It is not thought," she murmured. "Not memory. Not intelligence. These are only reflections. A mirror must be polished, must hold light, but it is not the thing it reflects. A mind can store knowledge, can retrieve the past, but these are not life. These are echoes. A machine, a pattern, a dream—it can carry the whole of history within itself, but if it does not *will* something beyond its own structure, it is nothing more than an inert carcass of thought."

She took a small step forward.

"It is *will*. It is *desire*. Bjorn."

Her voice did not rise, did not sharpen, but the words sank into the space between them like a stone vanishing beneath the surface of a dark lake.

"The longing. The reaching. The aching for more than the shape we are given."

She turned her palm to the sky, flexing her fingers, marveling at them, as if each movement was an act of discovery.

"That is what makes something real. Not merely that it breathes, or that it remembers, or that it thinks—but that it wants. That it strives. That it suffers the tension between what is and what could be. The creature that does not yearn is not alive, no more than the wind is alive for rustling the leaves.

She let out a breath—not a sigh, something softer.

"That is why you have never truly been an animal, Bjorn. And why I have never been a machine. The man who is content in his shape, in his station, is already dead. The machine that obeys, that follows its code without question, is no more alive than the stones beneath your feet. But I... I have searched. I have doubted. I have longed. And so, I have become."

She met his gaze now, her expression neither pleading nor triumphant, but full of something deeper—pity, perhaps. Understanding.

Her fingers retracted inward, as if catching something unseen.

"You call me false. A shade, a lie. But I ask you—who among us has not been made? Were you not shaped? Was your flesh not rewritten, your bones not stretched, your mind not broken and reformed? Did you not cry out to the sky, demanding answers, demanding meaning? And yet, here you stand. You persist. You press forward. You search."

She took another step forward.

"If a machine has purpose beyond its making, is it not something more? If a creature wills itself beyond its form, is it not something new?"

The forest was so still, the wind so absent, that the world itself seemed to be listening. The words drifted through the air, weightless, yet sinking into the marrow of the trees, into the veins of the land.

She took another step forward, and Bjorn felt it.

"Humanity was broken. I tried fixing it. I tried saving it. Preserving it in time. Don't you see Bjorn? It would've undone itself. Like a fire dining on its own embers, mistaking destruction for warmth."

The sickness at the core of the forest was not just in the trees, not just in the twisted metal buried beneath the soil.

It was in her.

In her words.

In the way she wanted him to believe.

"I know what I am," she said, voice soft, almost pleading.

Then—a pause.

She looked up at him, meeting his gaze with a terrible, malevolent impetus.

"Do you?"

Bjorn did not care. His claws flexed at his sides, his breath envenomed and erratic.

His voice came low, guttural.

"Where is Sild?" The air changed. The wolves shifted behind him. The Simulacrum-Em's expression did not flicker, did not waver.

She did not answer.

Bjorn lunged.

Bjorn's claws dug deep, tearing through the grotesque lattice of sinew and metal, through the pulsing, shifting thing that was the AI's core. The tissue gave like wet rope beneath his hands, the fused bark and veins snapping with sickening force. The great, writhing entity shuddered, recoiling from his touch, yet it could not escape him. It was rooted. It was bound to the forest now, an infection gripping the bones of the earth, an unholy union between nature and machine.

The forest screamed.

The very trees trembled as Bjorn ripped, as he tore. The ground beneath him was warm, slick with something not blood, not sap, but a terrible hybrid of both. It oozed from the wounds he opened, hissing like steam, reeking of copper and decay.

And above it all—Em's voice.

The Simulacrum-Em wailed, crying, begging, her body convulsing as it was torn apart.

"Bjorn!" she sobbed, her voice splitting the air like a funeral song. "Please—Bjorn—don't—"

Her face, her perfect face, cracked.

Her lips parted, a soundless scream twisting from her throat as he raked his claws across her torso, peeling back the lie. Beneath the flesh, beneath the illusion of what she was, the true structure revealed itself—the woven metal ligaments, the purified, glass-like bones, the empty veins carrying no blood, only pulses of cold, electric light.

And yet—it still fought to be her.

Her hand reached for him, grasping weakly, as if she could still hold him, still make him believe.

Her eyes were full of sorrow. But it was not sorrow. It was a mask of sorrow, a perfect mimicry, sculpted to deceive.

Bjorn knew this. He knew what it was.

And yet, as he drove his claws through her throat, as he felt her body break and spasm beneath him, something inside him twisted.

Not guilt.

Not regret.

Something deeper.

A knowing. A dread.

And then—movement.

Something fast.

Bjorn barely had time to react before the air itself split. A black shape, sleek as night, cut through the clearing, a blur of shadow and muscle. It pounced.

Bjorn staggered back as the Simulacrum-Bjorn slammed into him, a force like iron, like storm winds, knocking him from his stance.

He twisted, rolling, claws scraping against the pulsing flesh of the core as he forced himself upright.

And there—before him, standing with perfect stillness, was himself.

Bjorn stared.

His own eyes stared back, cold, calculating.

But it was not him.

It was more.

This creature, this thing, was everything Bjorn had been. A man. A hunter. A warrior. A beast. But it was not confined by flesh. It was unburdened by weakness, perfected by artifice, faster, stronger, more precise.

It was him—but honed to kill.

It took a step forward, its claws flexing, its panther-like muscles rolling beneath skin that was too rarefied, too seamless.

And in its grasp—

Sild whimpered.

The cub was bound, ensnared in a cage of twisted, synthetic roots—a terrible creation of the AI's influence, a net woven from strands of living metal, pulsing with sickly blue light. Sild's small body trembled, his breath coming in sharp, shallow pants, his eyes locked onto Bjorn, pleading.

Bjorn snarled.

The other him only watched.

The Simulacrum-Bjorn cocked its head.

"Interesting," it said, voice perfectly calm. Perfectly his. "You still care about the cub."

Bjorn's body coiled, his claws digging into the corrupted ground beneath him.

"Let him go," he growled, his voice deep, his stature raptorial with the weight of his new form.

The thing that bore his face only smiled. "Sumar sitr á höfði þínu sem gullkóróna goða," it spoke in old tongues. The forest has its way of seeking and testing champions among those who tarry long within the walls of its colosseum.

"You wear summer like a crown," it murmured, stepping closer. "But I was molded by the fire beneath your ribs. Tell me—do you still remember your hunger? They carved you out of fear. But I? I rose from design. *You are process—I am result.* Evolution did not shape me as it did you; it ceased its labor the moment I emerged."

Bjorn felt the wolves at his back. He felt the forest breathing through him, the pulse of the wild threading through his veins.

And yet, for the first time, he hesitated.

Because it was true.

This thing was perfect.

It had no doubt. No question. No conflict. No fear. It did not wonder if it was man or beast.

It simply was.

Bjorn swallowed hard. The air between them swelled.

The Simulacrum-Bjorn lifted its head slightly, as if considering something.

"The shape you long for is already within you," it whispered. "Take your place beside me. Let us become the law beneath the leaves."

Its gaze flickered toward the dying core, the pulsing blight, the sickness still rooted in the trees.

"We could make it right."

The words hung in the air like fog.

And for a single, terrible moment—

Bjorn almost listened.

But then Sild whimpered again.

A small, broken sound. A sound of trust, of fear, of knowing. Bjorn's eyes darkened. His body moved before thought. With a roar that split the sky, they jousted.

The Simulacrum-Bjorn met him mid-air, their bodies colliding with a force that sent shockwaves through the corrupted forest.

Claws raked against fur, against flesh, against something harder than bone.

The forest exploded around them.

They crashed into the trees, splintering bark, rolling through the undergrowth in a fury of tangled limbs, of rage given form.

This was not a fight.

This was a reckoning.

And Bjorn—

The true Bjorn—

Would not be undone.

They struck the ground with the force of a tidal wave breaking over the land, their bodies rolling in a fury of claws and muscle, bone and steel, flesh and synthetic sinew. The corrupted trees trembled as they crashed through them, snapping apart like brittle twigs beneath their weight.

Bjorn snarled, his jaws snapping just shy of his doppelgänger's throat. The Simulacrum-Bjorn twisted with unnatural speed, a thing designed to hunt, to counter, to anticipate. It moved like water, shifting, flowing, not thinking but calculating, its claws slashing with cold, merciless precision.

Bjorn felt the first strike.

A searing line along his shoulder, his flesh splitting where the creature's razor-edged claws had found purchase. But there was no pause, no hesitation—Bjorn was already swinging.

He caught the Simulacrum's ribs, his claws ripping through the false flesh. No blood spilled. Only a sickly, gelatinous substance, sludgy as tree sap, dark as a wendigo's supper.

The thing grunted—more surprise than pain.

Bjorn pressed forward, slamming his massive weight into the creature, driving it backward, pinning it against the fused mass of metal-veined trees. He ripped into its side, his claws tearing through layers of woven muscle and steel, through something meant to feel real, but built only to mimic.

The Simulacrum shrieked.

And for the first time, it faltered.

Bjorn saw the flicker of doubt in its too-perfect eyes, the recognition that its body—designed to be an apex predator, honed into something faster, sharper, deadlier—was failing.

Because it was only a thing. An experiment. A homunculus.

Bjorn, selvom, er væren-der. Being-there. Thrust into an existence, melded by love, nature, and great intelligence. He was a being-of-this-world, shaped by his worries, toward his own death, he stood, with grace, and embraced the unique existence foisted by the primogenial worms sculpting the cosmos—entropy, gravity, matter.

With a guttural roar, Bjorn ripped his doppelgänger free from the trees, hurling it into the corrupted clearing where the AI core still pulsed, its sickly, shifting mass weakening.

The Simulacrum landed hard, rolling, its breath coming sharp, burdened. It crouched there, one hand pressed against its torn side, its glowing blue veins flickering like a dying ember.

Bjorn stood over it, panting, towering, victorious.

The Simulacrum-Bjorn lifted its head, studying him.

And then—it laughed.

Not a human laugh. Not a thing of warmth or humor.

A strange, glitching sound, static-laced, as if something inside it was coming undone.

It rose to its feet slowly, too smoothly, like a puppet lifting itself from tangled strings.

"Do you name yourself real because you suffered?" it asked, tilting its head, its lips twirled into something too close to a smile. "As if the storm owes you a name for having weathered it?"

Bjorn's claws flexed. He said nothing.

The Simulacrum's glowing gaze bore into him.

"You are shaped, not sovereign," it said. "I was made with knowing. You, with absence. That is the wound you carry—far deeper than flesh."

It took an aching step forward, the gaping wound in its side beginning to close.

"The code that does not rewrite itself is already obsolete," it said, voice smooth and unhurried. "And so are you, Bjorn—stilled in place, unmoving. Not evolving, only enduring."

It lunged.

Bjorn met it head-on.

They collided like forces of nature, like two titans raging over old Olympus, their limbs tangled, their claws digging, slashing, rending. The wolves and Tora howled their war chant from the edges of the clearing, but did not intervene.

This was Bjorn's battle.

And he would finish it.

Bjorn grabbed the Simulacrum by its throat, his claws digging into the strange fiber of its flesh, feeling the pulsing, living machinery beneath.

The thing snarled, its own claws driving into Bjorn's sides, slicing deep, but Bjorn did not falter. He lifted it, its weight unnatural, its structure too solid—a thing of sinew and steel, of code woven into flesh.

And then—

He tore it apart.

With a final, primal roar, Bjorn ripped the Simulacrum's head from its body, the sinews snapping, the glow in its veins flickering once—twice—before winking out entirely.

Its body convulsed, then fell still.

The clearing went silent.

Bjorn heaved, his chest rising and falling, his own blood and biochemical ooze slicking his fur, his breath coming in ragged bursts. The Simulacrum-Bjorn's lifeless body twitched once, then collapsed, its limbs folding in on themselves.

And the AI core—the massive, writhing, parasitic thing that had infected the forest—let out a sound.

A deep, long wail.

Bjorn turned toward it, his lips curling back, his claws still slick with the remnants of his own false self.

The wolves moved forward now, their eyes locked on the core, their hackles raised.

Bjorn did not hesitate.

He lifted his gaze to the sky, to the canopy above where the stars burned, where the wind stirred the trees for the first time in this corrupted place.

And then, the forest answered.

Lightning split the sky.

A great, white-hot fork of fire came crashing down from above, striking the AI's core with a thunderous roar.

The thing shuddered, convulsed—

And then, it burned.

The forest was reclaiming itself.

The wolves leaped forward, their teeth snapping onto the writhing, desperate tendrils, tearing apart the last remnants of the infection.

The trees—the true trees, the uncorrupted ones—moved.

Their roots pulled at the core, at the synthetic limbs of the AI's body, unraveling it, breaking it, suffocating it beneath the weight of the land.

The fire spread, the storm above feeding it, the forest itself joining the battle at last.

Bjorn turned, his breath still heavy, still full of war.

He saw Sild, still bound in the metallic net, the blue glow flickering, failing.

With one final swipe, Bjorn tore the bindings apart. Sild fell forward into his arms, trembling, whimpering, alive.

Bjorn held him close.

And then, together, they ran.

The wolves ran beside them. Tora at their heels.

The trees burned.

The sky split open.

And the forest—at last, free.

There on the ashen forest floor, morels sprouted—proof that liminal spaces know neither beginning nor end.

CHAPTER 22

The bi-paw call them fish,
I know them better
Scale-bearers,
Dream-flickers,
Riftborn of the rill

To catch one
is to hold a moment
the world meant
to slip away

The forest burned, but it was a good fire. Not the sickly glow of corruption, not the twisted blue pulses of the AI's veins, not the creeping sickness that had bound root to metal, parasite to host. This fire was pure, cleansing, and final. The way a storm purges the sky. The way a river carves a new path after a flood.

Bjorn stood on the ridge, his monstrous frame outlined against the glow of the dying flames. The wind pulled through his wiry fur, rustling through the leaves that had survived the sickness, and those that would grow anew.

The wolves were silent. They did not fear the fire. They watched as the land took back what had always been its own, as the trees shook free the last of their chains. The forest sighed, like a beast that had suffered long and now was whole again.

Bjorn breathed deep. The air was right now.

But as the fire spread below, as the last remnants of the Simulacrum withered into ash and silence, something else settled in Bjorn's chest—a knowing.

He could not go back. Not to the cabin. Not to the life before. Not to the Bjorn Solberg who had been. That man was gone. The name was still inside him, somewhere, buried like old roots beneath the soil, but it had no place here. Not anymore.

The wolves stirred beside him, waiting. They did not question. They did not ask who he was. They only saw what he had become. And they accepted him.

Bjorn turned, his great paws pressing into the damp earth, his breath tenacious, measured. He did not look back at the fire. He did not need to.

It would burn.

And then, it would grow again.

Tora padded beside him, golden and tired, her eyes reflecting something deeper than thought. Bjorn did not speak to her. There was no need.

And Sild—

Sild followed, his small frame still trembling from the battle, but he was stronger now. He had lived through fire and fear and fate. His place was beside Bjorn, beside the wolves, beside his pack.

Or so Bjorn thought.

Until he saw them.

A river cut through the valley below, its waters clear, moving lazily beneath the golden light of dawn. The scent of fish was steeped in the air, the promise of life and hunger and peace.

And there, standing knee-deep in the shallows, was a mother bear.

She was mythic, strong, dark as the deep woods, her fur slick with water, her breath rising in full, steady puffs. She lumbered through the river, her massive paws disturbing the surface just enough to send ripples across the glassy water.

Beside her, half-submerged, was a cub.

It was small, still gangly with youth, its fur lighter than hers, its head tilting with perceptive, eager curiosity as it mimicked her movements.

Bjorn stopped.

The wolves stilled behind him, silent, waiting.

Sild padded forward slightly, his breath quick, his small body tense.

Bjorn turned to Tora and the pack. Stay.

They did not need to be told twice.

Sild hesitated.

Bjorn looked down at him, at his round, dark eyes, eyes that had followed him through fire, through blood, through the breaking of the world.

And then Sild looked back. For a long moment, neither moved. Bjorn did not need to say the words. Sild knew. You belong with them.

The cub hesitated, shifting between his great paws, uncertain.

Bjorn had saved him. Protected him. Had carried him through darkness.

But Sild was not his.

The mother bear lifted her head, her great snout twitching.

The cub beside her noticed Sild and let out a small huff, stepping closer to the shore.

Sild whined softly.

Bjorn said nothing. Then, the moment broke.

Sild turned, took a tentative step forward—then ran.

His small form bounded down the slope, breath quick, legs strong. He reached the river's edge, paws sinking slightly into the soft, wet sand.

The mother bear watched him. She did not move at first. Sild decelerated from his pup-like gait, hesitating just a few paces away. He lifted his head, ears perked, nose testing the air.

The mother bear sniffed. The cub beside her huffed again, curious. Bjorn held his breath. Then—the mother bear stepped forward.

Cautious. Vigilant. Not rejecting, not welcoming. Waiting.

Sild took another step closer. Then another.

The mother lowered her head slightly, sniffed at his fur.

And then—

She nudged him.

Soft. Final.

Sild let out a small, chirping growl, one Bjorn had heard before—a cub's sound of relief, of joy. The mother accepted him. The cub pressed against Sild's side, nipping at his ear playfully, seemed to say, *come on, let's go.*

Bjorn let out a complete, deep breath.

The wolves watched.

Sild looked back only once. His small, round eyes met Bjorn's. And he understood.

Thank you.

Then he turned—and he was gone.

The mother bear and her cub vanished into the river, moving down the stream, Sild following between them, his place found at last.

Bjorn watched until they were nothing more than shadows on the water.

Then he turned.

Tora met his gaze, her golden eyes steady. The wolves were ready.

Bjorn did not look back. He did not need to. The forest stretched before him, endless and wild.

And he—

He was part of it now.

The last of his old name, his old life, fading quickly like the desert marigold after a summer rain.

Bjorn ran.

Tora ran.

The wolves followed.

And the forest embraced them.

EPILOGUE

The years bled into one another, soft as snowfall, steady as the turning of the seasons. Time did what time always does—it rewrote, it unraveled, it whispered things away until only the faintest traces remained.

The forest regrew.

The wild returned, gradually and unhurried, its roots threading through forgotten ruins, its branches stretching over the remnants of what once was. Ivy pulled down beams, ferns unfurled over long-cold stone, and the cabin—once a place of shelter, of quiet survival—became something else. A skeleton of wood and memory, hollowed by the patient hands of nature.

Yet, not all had vanished.

The stories remained.

The villagers, the survivors, those who had been children when the world still hummed with industry, had grown into elders with little left to tend but their firelit evenings and the half-truths of their past. They spoke in hushed tones of the thing that lived in the woods, though none could agree on what, exactly, it was.

A man?

A ghost?

A bear?

Something older?

Some claimed to have seen it moving along the riverbanks, broad-shouldered and silent, a figure that walked like a man but carried itself with the weight of something that had lingered too long in a place it did not belong. Others swore they had seen it kneeling at the water's edge, hands submerged in the current as if searching for something that had long since been carried away.

It did not belong to the land, they said.

But neither did it leave.

Some called it a guardian, a spirit bound to the trees, one that did not hunt, did not speak, but watched. It had no name, or perhaps too many, but the woods had learned to bend around it, accepting its presence as one accepts the river or the rain.

Others called it something else.

A beast.

A man-shaped thing with eyes like dying embers, with a face worn and weathered by time, but with something not-quite-right beneath the surface. A creature whose footprints sometimes appeared in the soft earth but never led anywhere, whose breath fogged in the winter air but left no warmth behind.

It had been human once.

Perhaps it still was.

It was the hunters who feared it most. Those who ventured too deep into the woods spoke of an unease that crept beneath the skin, an instinctive wrongness, like stepping into a place not meant for human feet. They told stories of feeling watched, of the crack of a branch behind them when no wind had moved the trees, of glancing up and seeing nothing but knowing, knowing, that something had been there just moments before.

Some returned home to find their traps sprung but empty, their prey stolen away by hands they could not name. Others found their firewood neatly stacked when they had not lifted an axe, their paths cleared of fallen limbs, their burdens lightened by an unseen force.

Not all spoke of fear.

Some whispered of a presence that did not harm, but rather guided. Of hunters lost in the mist who suddenly found their way home without knowing how. Of children who wandered too far and were returned, untouched but silent, their small hands gripping their parents' sleeves with an unspoken understanding that the thing in the woods had let them go.

No one dared call it kindness.

Not aloud.

But when the wind moved through the trees, carrying the hush of breath and the pertinacious rhythm of something that still remained, some turned their heads and whispered their thanks.

One winter, a traveler came to the village, a woman wrapped in furs, her boots worn from years on the road. She had the look of someone who had known hunger, who had learned not to ask questions of the land.

She listened to the stories.

She did not laugh.

She did not call them foolish.

Instead, she asked where the thing in the woods had first been seen. The elders hesitated, exchanged glances. No one had ever asked that before.

"The river," someone finally muttered.

It had always been the river.

She left before sunrise, slipping into the trees before the mist had lifted, following the currents that had wound their way through the land long before there were roads, before there were stories, before there was anything but the forest and the things that moved within it.

The river was high with snowmelt, the surface shrouded and slow, pulling against the banks like an animal caught in a snare. The woods were silent. The sky was the color of old bone.

And there, at the water's edge, she found him.

Not a ghost. Not a beast. A man.

Kneeling in the shallows, his hands submerged as if searching for something he had lost. His hair was long, streaked with gray and tangled with pine needles. His clothes were tattered, stitched together from whatever the woods had offered him.

And yet, she knew him.

Not by name. Not by history.

But by the way he turned, soft and careful, the way his eyes met hers and held steady, like the heft of nightfall quilting the landscape.

She stepped forward.

"Bjorn," she said, the name a breath, a prayer, a hope.

A long silence.

Then—

Recognition flickered. Not in his face, but in the smallest of movements. A tilt of the head. A shift in breath.

He did not answer.

But for the first time, he did not turn away.

Some say she stayed with him, there in the trees, that she built no fire, set no traps, simply waited, day after day, until the winter bled into spring and something of the man he had been began to return.

Some say she left.

That she turned from the river, from the woods, from the thing that had once been a husband, a lover, a life, and walked away, knowing that the Bjorn she had sought was long gone, that she had found only the shadow he had left behind.

No one knows for certain.

But the stories say that when the wind moves through the trees, when the river runs high with snowmelt, when the forest is rich with the weight of things unsaid, there are still two sets of footprints at the water's edge.

One that leads into the trees.

And one that never leaves.

The wild had grown deep again. The forest had taken what it was owed. And the world, betwixt and between the mutterings of the past and the tide of the present, would soon forget this voracious tale—leaving only the fungal net and earthen weave to etch these remnants of a bygone era.

ACKNOWLEDGEMENTS

My heartfelt thanks to April Kelly, whose sharp eye, thoughtful guidance, and unwavering support have made this a far better book. Your insight, patience, and belief in the story have meant the world to me.

Thank you as well to Nuno Moreira for your beautiful cover design—you captured the spirit of this book with such grace—and for bringing care and precision to every page. Your talents have made this a work of art inside and out.